Badger, Beano
& the
Magic Mushroom

Badger, Beano & the Magic Mushroom

Jack Scoltock

Illustrated by Jeanette Dunne

WOLFHOUND PRESS

First published in Ireland 1990 by
WOLFHOUND PRESS
68 Mountjoy Square, Dublin 1.

Published in Great Britain 1991

British Library Cataloguing in Publication Data
Scoltock, Jack
    Badger, beano and the magic mushroom.
    I. Title
    823.914 [J]

    ISBN 0-86327-263-0

Wolfhound Press receives financial assistance from The Arts Council (An Chomhairle Ealaíon), Dublin, Ireland.

Cover illustration: Jeanette Dunne
Cover design: Jan de Fouw
Typesetting: Seton Graphics, Bantry.
Printed by The Guernsey Press Co. Ltd., Channel Islands.

For Ursula
with love

Chapter One

They called him Badger, because his hair was black—and from the middle of his forehead, just above his big brown eyes, to the middle of the back of his head, a two centimetre band of white hair grew.

Richard Phelan was his real name. He lived with his father in the little Irish town of Kilkee. Richard's mother, who died soon after he was born, had had a similar white streak in her hair.

Badger was a strange boy. He had no real friends and most of the boys and girls in the town avoided him. But the animals now. They were different. Badger seemed to have some strange power over them. They liked him. It was as simple as that.

One Saturday morning Badger's father hurried down Castle Street, on his way to the butchers. What he saw in the pet-shop window that day was to change his son's life. It was a collie dog. Black all over, but for a white band of hair that grew from its black nose, right along its back, where it fanned out onto its long tail.

As Mr Phelan stared through the window at the dog, something strange happened. Somehow, he felt he had to buy the dog for his son.

Ten minutes later, he headed home with the dog trotting happily beside him on a new leather leash.

'Look what I've bought you,' he announced when he arrived home. Badger was delighted. A dog of his very own!

Badger looked at his father, then at the dog, and a name came to him immediately.

7

'BEANO!' he cried, and the dog jumped into his open arms and began licking him all over his face.

Badger's father smiled as he watched them. Now maybe he'll talk to me and tell me what he's thinking. Maybe this will bring us closer together, he thought.

Badger and Beano became inseparable. They went everywhere together, even to school where Beano would wait patiently outside for class to finish. Then came the time when all this changed.

On the first Sunday of the summer holidays their adventure began. An adventure so strange that if Badger told anyone about it, they wouldn't have believed him. In fact, they would have thought he was crazy.

Rising early, Badger looked out of the window. It was a warm sunny day. He dressed quickly in his blue jeans, striped runners and plain white tee-shirt. He slipped quietly down the stairs so as not to wake his father.

Out in the back yard he fed Beano. Whistling happily he watched Beano wolf down his food. But, he failed to see two strange looking birds sitting on the branch of a tree, watching him. 'Is this the day the Grey One is to go to the land of Beyond?' one of the birds chirped in its own language.

'Aye,' the other replied, his beady eyes watching Badger and Beano intently. 'Him and his Familiar . . . Beano? Isn't that the four-legged creature's name?'

The birds watched as Badger went inside and returned with a bowl of water for Beano.

'I hope they can save the land,' one of the birds said. 'It is written in the great book that they will. Everything written in the great book has to come true . . . ,' the other bird nodded in agreement.

As Beano lapped up the cold water, Badger gazed at the green hills above the town. The sky was cloudless. It would be a good day to explore the hills, he thought. Turning to Beano he said, 'Beano, I think we'll go exploring in the hills today, what do you think, eh, boy?' Beano barked happily. Twenty minutes later they were heading towards the windy path at the back of the housing estate which led to the hills.

Up, up, up, they went. Eventually they came to the end of the path, and then began to climb the steeper rocky way to the highest point of the hills. When they reached the top after about thirty minutes, they sat on the smooth grass to rest, as Badger was out of breath, his face aglow, and Beano was panting heavily, his long pink tongue falling from his mouth.

Looking over the valley Badger could see flashes below them, as window panes in the town glinted in the sun. The river Brack wended its way through the valley along the south side of Kilkee.

Just below the hill they were on, was a small wood.

'Come on, Beano! Let's go down there.' Badger shouted excitedly.

Minutes later they reached it and walked around the edge looking for a way in.

'It's very dark in there, Beano,' Badger whispered, peering into the dark wood. They didn't know that they were being observed by two brown rabbits with white bushy tails. With his nose wrinkling in excitement one rabbit said to the other, 'Are you sure I'll be alright?'

'Of course you will. Just show yourself to the Familiar, and then head for the clearing. Sure he'll never catch you.'

Taking a few deep breaths the white breasted rabbit scudded out of the trees, and stood up directly in front of Beano. Beano's ears pricked up, and his eyes grew wider. Before he could react the rabbit raced into the trees and Beano sped into the undergrowth after it.

'Beano, come back!' yelled Badger amazed. 'Come back . . . at once!' Still shouting, he followed the sound of Beano's barking deep into the wood.

'So now it begins,' chirped one of the birds who had been watching them earlier.

'Aye. He will fulfil his destiny this day.'

Chapter Two

Deeper and deeper into the dark wood ran Badger, still following the sound of Beano's barking. Suddenly he came to a clearing.

It was as big as the inside of Kilkee Chapel. Tiny shafts of sunlight beamed through the thick foliage of the trees onto the leafy ground. Microscopic pieces of dust and wood creatures rode on the beams. Butterflies fluttered here and there, searching for somewhere to rest. A bee buzzed past Badger's ear as it fled back into the trees.

At first Badger didn't see what Beano was facing. But a broad shaft of sunlight suddenly shone down, revealing the biggest mushroom Badger had ever seen. Beano seemed hypnotised. His mouth was open, and his red quivering tongue glistened with saliva as he stared up at the giant mushroom. Badger walked slowly towards Beano without taking his eyes off the mushroom. He whispered,

'Come on boy. Easy now. Come on, let's go. . . .'

As he straightened up, he realised that the mushroom was now about three times taller than himself. Freckles the size of his hand flickered along its smooth umbrella. The stem of the mushroom was as thick as his Dad's body.

'Hallo Badger. You've come then. . . .'

A singing, booming, crystal clear voice sounded around the clearing, Beano rose to his feet and stood beside his master.

'Eh?'

Badger looked all around him. He could see no one. They must be hiding in the trees, he thought.

'Aren't you going to say hallo, then?' The booming, singing voice spoke again.

Once more Badger searched the edge of the clearing. He could see no one. As Beano began licking at his hand, the mushroom shook slightly, and then turned a bright orange colour.

'Aren't you going to say hallo, Grey One?'

Badger gaped as he suddenly realised that it was the mushroom speaking.

'You . . .' stuttered Badger. 'It's you who is singing. A . . . A . . mushroom. . . . !'

'Yes . . . I'm a mushroom. But I'm not an ordinary mushroom. Oh no indeed, Grey One. I'm a magic mushroom.'

'Magi . . . magic . . . mush . . .' gulped Badger, backing away, staring as its brown freckles began to flicker ever more quickly.

'Yes, I am a magic mushroom. Oh really, Grey One, I had hoped for a more intelligent response to me. Your dog . . . Beano . . . yes, that's his name. He has told me all about you.'

'Beano . . . ?' stammered Badger. 'He told you all about me?'

'Yes, but I knew about you already.'

Badger looked down at his dog, and Beano raised his white streaked head. For a second Badger could have sworn Beano gave him a knowing wink. In a daze he looked at the mushroom again.

'What do you mean, you knew all about me?' he asked.

'It was foretold in the great book.'

'Look, mushroom!' Badger shouted, no longer afraid. 'What's this all about? Who are you really? What are you doing in this wood?'

For a few moments the mushroom's freckles whizzed all over its umbrella. Then it said, 'Which question would you like me to answer first?'

'Well . . . Tell me, what you are doing in this wood?'

'Oh I've always lived here,' the mushroom sang in a soothing tone. 'You see I am the gateway to the land of Beyond.'

'The what?'

'The land of Beyond.'

'Beyond? Beyond what?'

'Beyond time. In another place. A different dimension, if you like.'

Badger tried to digest the meaning of the mushroom's words.

'Maybe I should begin at the beginning,' said the mushroom. 'A very good place to start. Perhaps you had better sit down, Grey One.'

Defiantly, Badger stood perfectly still.

The mushroom shook violently for a few seconds, then sang in a deep, low voice.

'Oh I see, that's how it is, is it? Very well then. Stand and I'll explain.'

At once, Badger sat down. The mushroom shook even more violently, the colour of his umbrella changing to a deep red, then blue, then bluer still until it became almost purple.

'Oh dear . . . Oh dear . . .' It sang in a low mournful voice. 'I'll have to control myself. I'd need. . . .'

'Look, mushroom!' Badger shouted. 'I want to know what this is all about. We'll have to be getting home soon as we've been gone all morning.'

'Yes, yes, I'm sorry Grey One. I'll continue, but please do not interrupt me. I need to concentrate.'

'Well, get on with it!' Badger interrupted loudly.

The mushroom shook violently and changed from purple to different shades of green, fading into white. Badger and his dog could hear it breathing heavily as it tried to control itself.

'Please. . . please. . . you'll upset me. I'll not be right . . .',

'Will you hurry up.' Badger snapped. 'What are you trying to say?'

Taking a few quick breaths, the mushroom shook itself and chanted: 'In the beginning it was foretold in the great book that a boy with a white streak in his hair would save the land of Beyond. It must be you for you have the mark.'

'Save the land of Beyond? What do you mean?'

'What I said. He would save the land of Beyond.'

'From what? . . .'

'May I please continue?' the mushroom asked, its voice growing deeper and sounding as if it was going to lose its temper.

'Yes, yes of course you can. Who's stopping you?'

'You are! You . . . Oh Grey One, don't make me angry again. I hate myself when I get angry. I don't feel right for years after. . . .'

'Look mushroom!' Badger shouted. 'Never mind all that. How was it foretold that I would save the land of Beyond? Tell me.'

Beano looked up at his master, then at the mushroom, and back to his master again.

Taking a long deep breath the mushroom continued.

'You see Grey One, there are many lands in other times in other dimensions. A rift, a tear appeared in the time zone that leads to the land of Beyond. Evil beings of the ancient Irish, and the Evil one himself, have entered the land.'

Pausing, the mushroom shook for a few moments before continuing. 'The rift is healed again, and now the only entrance to the land of Beyond is through me. I have been asked to allow you to enter. You, and your Familiar, Beano. He will be of great help to you there.'

Badger looked at Beano, and once again Beano winked at him. Turning to the mushroom, Badger asked, 'This land of Beyond, where is it?'

To Badger's astonishment, the giant mushroom slowly began to sink into the ground until only its umbrella remained above the surface. Then it split in half to reveal a row of tiny steps leading down into darkness.

'Why not enter and see for yourself, Grey One?' the mushroom sang.

'Down there . . . ?' gulped Badger, stretching his neck to see where the steps led.

Suddenly, Beano jumped towards the steps and disappeared below.

'Come on master!' Badger heard him shout.

'Is . . . is that really you, Beano?' Badger stammered.

Beano's voice echoed from the darkness, 'Yes master. Come on. You know it's O.K. Come on. . . .'

Strangely Badger didn't feel afraid, he knew he would be safe with Beano although he didn't understand how Beano could suddenly talk to him.

'Hold on, Beano. I'm coming. Wait for me . . . I'm coming.'

Chapter Three

Down, down, down he stumbled, holding onto the spongy sides of the dark interior. He felt his runners sink into the spongy steps. Below him now he could see a tunnel of light. Soon he reached the bottom. Beano was waiting at a half open door. Above it were the words, WELCOME TO THE LAND OF BEYOND. The letters were formed by a family of glow worms. Beyond what? thought Badger as he pushed the door open wider and followed Beano through. He saw another row of steps that led up, up, up, and then in the dim light he saw them disappear around a corner. In a flash Beano was leaping up the steps.

'Wait for me!' Badger shouted, hurrying up after him.

A minute later, Badger and Beano climbed the last two spongy steps and came out of the mushroom. Turning, they saw it close up and then rise to its full height again.

Looking around him Badger saw that they were in the same clearing . . . Except . . . Except. . . .

High above him, birds of a million varieties sang happily in the trees. But these were not ordinary trees. Their leaves were as colourful as the birds. And the smells . . . beautiful scents of millions of flowers drifted to him. A green mist ankle deep clung to the floor of the clearing. Even stranger than this was the fact that he felt ecstatically happy. Beano sniffed happily at his feet.

'Am I here? Is this the land of Beyond?' Badger asked turning to the mushroom.

'Of course,' it answered, its voice sweet and melodic. 'Don't you feel happy?'

'Yes, yes I do,' Badger smiled.

'Me too, master,' Beano said, looking up at him.

'Beano, can you really talk? I mean, is it really you?'

'Yes master,' Beano replied woofing twice to show his master the difference.

Turning back to the mushroom Badger asked, 'Where do we go from here?'

'Wait here for a little while. Someone who has been guarding the belt of the Ancients will welcome you. When it is offered, you must take it. Without the belt you would have little chance against the evil ones. It really belongs to you, you see.'

'A belt?'

'The belt of the Ancients. A magic belt.'

'Magic belt,' Badger whispered looking at Beano.

Just then, a rope made of thick grass dropped to the ground from the trees and a little man slid down, landing lightly beside them.

'I'd like you to meet your guide. The great Macgillycuddy, Lord of all the little people in Ireland. He has come bearing a gift for you,' the mushroom explained.

Badger and Beano gaped at the little man, for he was truly little. From his tiny feet to the top of his tassled cap he only came to Badger's knees. He wore knee length boots with pointed toes, and a light long john made from many pieces of badger skin. He scowled at them through his bushy grey beard which fell below his waist. His angular ears stuck up past the rim of his woollen cap. Around his waist was a thick belt fastened with a gold buckle in the shape of a shamrock. A tiny shillelagh hung on one side and a black leather bag on the other.

'So this is the chosen one? The Grey One?' he asked, and Badger saw his sharp pointed yellow teeth.

'For you to find out, Macgillycuddy. Have you brought the belt of the Ancients?' the mushroom sang.

'Of course I have,' scowled the little man. 'Sure haven't I been guarding it for nigh on five hundred years?'

Badger looked down at Beano. 'Guarding it for five hundred years,' he thought to himself.

'A long time, master,' he heard Beano thinking.

Badger gaped down at his dog, astonished. 'Can you read my thoughts too, Beano?' he asked silently.

'It appears so, master,' Beano replied wordlessly.

Then with two gnarled fingers, Macgillycuddy reached into the leather bag and withdrew a strange belt. It was completely white, except for some green writing which Badger could not understand. The curious buckle on the belt was in the shape of a harp, and it had a red diamond about the size of a penny fixed to it which began to glow.

Swinging the belt around, the leprechaun shouted, 'Hold up your hands, Grey One! Hold up your hands and receive the belt of the Ancients which I have guarded with my life these five centuries!'

Suddenly with a quick throw the little man launched the belt into the air. Up, up, into the trees it soared until it was lost among the branches. For a moment Badger lowered his hands.

'Keep your hands up, Grey One!' Macgillycuddy shouted. 'You must keep them up to be able to receive the belt of the Ancients.'

Badger, Beano and Macgillycuddy looked into the trees, and in amazement they saw the belt come into sight again. Then it began to drift downwards until it hovered over Badger's hands. The diamond had changed colour. It was now a burning cobalt blue. Faster and faster the belt began to revolve. Beano saw his master rise slowly off the ground. Then the belt looped over his head and settled down onto his waist. Badger was held there for a few seconds and he felt the magical power of the belt surge through him. Then he floated down beside Beano again. He stood with an amazed expression on his face.

'Are you O.K. master?' thought Beano, looking up at him.

'I think so, Beano. Yes, I'm fine. In fact I feel wonderful,' he laughed. Then the mushroom spoke again.

'Well, Grey One, that's good. Now I can return, for my part in this is finished. Macgillycuddy will tell you the rest. It just remains for me to say good luck. Not that luck will come into it, mind you. One thing to remember, beware of Mefistofelees, the Evil One. He knows you are here now. Beware of false friends too. Trust no one, only your Familiar and Macgillycuddy. . . .'

As the mushroom began to sink into the ground Badger shouted, 'Tell me before you go. How am I to look for these evil ones? What do I have to do? How will I find them?'

As the mushroom disappeared from sight the last words it sang were, 'THEY WILL FIND YOU. THEY HAVE TO DESTROY YOU . . . goodbye and good luck.'

Then it was gone. Badger and Beano stared at the ground where the mushroom had been. Their thoughts were interrupted by Macgillycuddy saying,

'It's time we moved out of these trees, they know we are here. We will have to move quickly. It is growing dark and the wind is starting.'

Badger noted the worried expression on his face.

They followed the leprechaun across the clearing and into the trees. The wind grew even stronger, blowing leaves and twigs into their faces. Beano shivered as he kept close to his master.

'At the edge of the trees there is a mist,' Macgillycuddy shouted, trying to make himself heard above the sound of the wind. 'We must reach there quickly.'

Behind them they heard a crash.

'What was that? ' Badger yelled.

'A falling tree I think,' Macgillycuddy answered, turning to him. 'Hurry, we must continue on. When we reach the mist we will be safe. I have a unicorn waiting for us there. Hurry. . . .'

They heard more loud crashes. The awful sound was coming closer.

'That's not trees falling, Macgillycuddy!' cried Badger, his hands protecting his face as he tried to keep the stinging leaves from hitting it. 'Where is the edge of the wood? Do you know the way at all?'

'It's this way . . . I . . . I . . . think,' the little man shouted uncertainly, still darting on.

The crashing sounds came nearer and nearer. Then they heard the most terrible roar.

'Macgillycuddy, where are we?' screamed Badger.

In the very dim light Badger saw the terrified look on the little leprechaun's face, and he knew that Macgillycuddy didn't know where they were.

Suddenly, Badger felt very heavy, and looking down he saw the belt glowing. Before he realised what he was doing his hand shot out and a broad beam of light burst from it, lighting up the darkness ahead.

'I see the way now, Grey One!' shouted Macgillycuddy. 'This way . . . follow me . . . quickly. . . .'

Almost tripping over the little man, Badger and Beano hurried after him onto a narrow path. 'It's just a bit further on. We're nearly there. . . .'

At last they came running out of the trees and into a bright tingling mist. They listened, but whatever had been chasing them had gone.

'Where are we now, Macgillycuddy?' Badger asked, looking at the belt as it stopped glowing.

'We are near Ceancasslagh. You'll see it shortly. Come this way.'

As they followed the leprechaun and emerged from the mist, Macgillycuddy pointed saying, 'There. The land of Beyond.'

Chapter Four

What Badger saw as they looked down on the valley of Ceancasslagh took his breath away. A silver river, bordered on both sides
by fields and fields of flowers of every colour, eased its winding way
through the valley. It must be the flowers that are making the land
smell so sweet, he thought. The leaves on the trees were multi-
coloured. There was a pinky brightness everywhere, even in the
fluffy clouds. Thousands of beautiful butterflies fluttered about the
fields, sometimes stopping to rest on the flowers. The sound of
humming bees gorging themselves on nectar filled the air.

As they followed Macgillycuddy down through the fields, they
saw apples, bananas, pears, and oranges the size of footballs, all
growing together on the same tree. Further down they came to a
tall tree that housed hundreds of many-coloured birds. Their
singing was so relaxing to listen to. Badger smiled as he saw two of
the tiny birds with red and blue wings land on Macgillycuddy's
cap. Another one landed on Badger's shoulder. Just as it did, he felt
the belt vibrate. Looking down he saw that the diamond was
glowing, only this time it was black. Beano growled as he thought,
'Master, I smell danger, something evil.'

Looking around him, Badger could see nothing that looked
dangerous. Only the beautiful countryside and the birds.

Suddenly, magical power surged up his left arm and into his
head. Three beams of magic immediately burst from his eyes. Two
of the beams knocked the birds from Macgillycuddy's head. The

third beam swung around in an arc and hit the bird that was closest to Badger's neck.

As all three birds hit the ground, they changed with a quick burst of evil magic into the three leprechauns that they really were.

'MEFISTOES!' shouted Macgillycuddy, brandishing his shillelagh.

These leprechauns didn't look at all like Macgillycuddy. They had hairy legs and two cloven feet like a goat. They wore trousers made of a canvas material that showed their knobbly knees. Two of the evil little men wore red waistcoats made from pieces of leather sewn together. Under the waistcoat they wore a sort of polo-neck tee-shirt, which exposed their short muscular hairy arms. Around their waists in a wide leather belt, each had a long curved dagger with a diamond encrusted handle. The third leprechaun wore a black waistcoat made from otterskins over a white polo-neck tee-shirt. But the most horrible things about these evil little men was that their grotesque heads were matted with long, dirty black hair from which grew several short black horns and that their teeth were pointed and very sharp. Screaming with anger they snatched out their daggers. In a flash Beano was into them, his sharp teeth ripping at their legs. A blue glow surrounded him and the fierce stabs that the Mefistoes made bounced harmlessly off him. Crying with pain they retreated.

'Stop! Stop! Have mercy!' the Mefisto with the black waistcoat screamed. 'Call off your Familiar . . . ahhh. . . .'

'Familiar! I hate being called that!' Beano barked, taking a bite from the leprechaun's hairy leg.

'Beano!' shouted Badger. 'Here boy. Here, let them go. . . .'

With an angry growl Beano reluctantly returned to his master's side. Now Macgillycuddy began screaming as he jumped up and down.

'Kill them! Kill them! You must kill them! They tried to kill us. . . .'

'Kill them?' Badger said, horrified at the prospect. 'Why I couldn't. No . . . I . . . I. . . .'

'You must! They will warn the others. They will tell their evil leader Mefistofelees that you are here. They have to try and kill you for you are the only threat to their tyranny in the land of Beyond. You have to kill them!'

'But this Mefistofelees knows I'm here anyway. No . . . no, I won't kill them,' argued Badger.

Badger was standing with his back to the Mefistoes and Beano lay on the ground dripping saliva while watching them. Slowly, clutching their daggers they crept towards Badger.

'Master,' thought Beano. 'They are creeping up behind you.'

Without even turning around, Badger felt the magic from the belt of the Ancients engulf him. From the back of his head, three pencil thin beams of magic shot out and hit the Mefistoes' daggers. With painful cries as the metal melted all over their hands they turned and ran down through the flowers. They passed a unicorn who was galloping up through the fields towards Badger and the others. With a loud welcome 'neigh' he stopped before them, snorting and puffing.

Badger and Beano gazed in wonder at the beautiful creature that was slightly smaller than an ordinary horse. The unicorn looked at them with big black eyes. It was completely white even to the long pointed horn that grew from just above its eyes.

Smiling, Macgillycuddy patted it on the side.

'Let me introduce you to Caliopes, Lord of the unicorns,' he said.

'I say, pleased to meet you chaps,' the unicorn said, swinging its head up and down excitedly. With a smile Badger held out his hand.

'Pleased to meet you, Cal, Cal?'

'Caliopes, old boy. So you are the Badger, what?'

'Badger, yes, I'm called Badger.'

Beano stared up at the unicorn, and whispered, 'a bit of a rare one this, master.'

Badger smiled.

'Rare one!' Caliopes snorted. 'Of course I'm a rare one. It's not every day you get to meet the lord of the unicorns, is it, what?'

'Enough of this,' Macgillycuddy said sharply. 'Come, Caliopes, kneel down and allow us to mount you. We have to get down below quickly.'

Neighing loudly, Caliopes bent his two front legs and lowered his majestic head. With a quick leap Macgillycuddy was on his back and sitting just above the tail. Seconds later, Badger scrambled up beside him.

'Your Familiar can run beside us, Grey One.' Macgillycuddy said. Before Badger could say anything, Beano growled, 'Look, little man. My name is Beano . . . Beano! I'm not Familiar . . . and yes I will run beside you, because I choose to. . . .'

Badger smiled, then he felt the belt vibrating.

'We'd better get on our way, Macgillycuddy. The belt of the Ancients is warning me of danger.'

Above them in the mist, three cloaked wraith-like beings watched them. They were so enveloped that it was hard to see where the mist ended and their forms began. As Caliopes galloped down the fields carrying Badger and the Leprechaun, with Beano running behind them, the cloaked figures drifted into the sky and disappeared.

Chapter Five

'Where are we going, Mac?' Badger shouted. He had decided to shorten Macgillycuddy's name. The little man looked irritated as he answered,

'We have to make our way along the edge of the river Faughan and hope we can get to the village of the golden ones. They had a visit from the evil ones. A task will be waiting for you there.'

'Golden ones? A task? What do you mean?' asked Badger frowning.

'Listen to me, Grey One,' Macgillycuddy whispered, his face looking even more grim as he bounced up and down on Caliopes' back, 'our first encounter with the Mefistoes was to try you out. Their next attack will not be as easy to ward off. You will have to kill them. . . .'

'No! No!' Badger shouted, 'I will not kill. It is wrong.'

'Pish pshaw!' exclaimed Macgillycuddy angrily. 'What the evil one and his minions are doing to the land of Beyond is wrong. As you encounter these evil Mefistoes you must destroy them, or they will eventually destroy you.'

Badger grew even angrier.

'Look, Macgillycuddy, what is wrong with this land? All I've seen has been beautiful, except for the three mefistoes. There seems to be very little wrong here. No, I will not kill. Evil cannot be conquered by using evil. So let me hear no more from you about killing. Do you understand, Macgillycuddy? Do you?'

'Pish pshaw!' the leprechaun exclaimed turning away, his beard bristling with anger.

Ten miles further on, they came to a bend. Caliopes neighed loudly and abruptly halted, almost knocking Badger and Macgillycuddy off his back. Ahead, blocking their way, were six huge rocks. Badger felt the belt vibrate and noticed it was glowing black.

'Get down, Mac,' he whispered. 'We will approach those rocks on foot. The belt is warning me there is danger.'

'We could go around the rocks, Grey One,' Macgillycuddy whispered, his voice shaking with fear.

'No, whatever danger there is has to be faced. The mushroom told me the evil will find me. So why avoid it?'

Macgillycuddy looked up at Badger's face, then shook his head.

'Beano,' Badger whispered. 'Watch out. Caliopes, you stay here.'

'Whatever you say, old bean,' the unicorn whispered, bending its beautiful head and tearing at some dew soaked grass.

With Beano just a little ahead of them, Badger and the leprechaun edged cautiously towards the rocks.

'Something doesn't smell right, master,' sniffed Beano. 'In fact, whatever it is smells downright rotten.'

'Be alert, Beano,' Badger thought. Macgillycuddy drew his shillelagh.

The rock five metres away from them suddenly burst apart. Thick green burning lava began to gush from it. Now in quick succession the other rocks exploded, oozing smoking lava. In seconds a river of burning death rushed towards them destroying everything in its path.

'Look out!' Badger shouted. 'The wall of lava is going to engulf us.' Badger touched the magic buckle on his belt and two beams surrounded Beano and Macgillycuddy. In no time they were hovering above the lava, beside him.

'Run Caliopes! Run!' Badger ordered. The unicorn saw the danger coming towards him and with a loud snort he galloped away.

'Don't worry about us, Caliopes,' Badger shouted. 'We'll see you later.'

When Macgillycuddy looked at Badger, he noticed his eyes were glowing a bright yellow and the white hair on his head was standing straight up. Seconds later Badger's power landed them on the path fifty metres ahead of the shattered rocks.

'The belt of the Ancients has great magic, Grey One,' Macgilly-cuddy smiled. 'We were lucky that time. . . .'

'No,' Badger said quietly, looking at Beano who winked at him. 'It was not luck, I knew what I was doing.'

Back in the trees a dark figure of unspeakable evil reached out and ripped a beautiful tree out of the ground and flung it furiously aside. Then with a loud curse he disappeared.

'It looks like we'll be travelling on foot from now on, master,' Beano thought. 'Do you want me to check up ahead?'

'No stay with us. I can hear voices up ahead.'

Beano's ears shot up, and tilting his white streaked head he listened, but could hear nothing.

Chapter Six

One mile on, the path dipped into a small valley. Looking down they saw a village where hundreds of beautiful children waited patiently. When they saw Badger and the rest they cheered loudly and began running towards them.

'Who are they?' Badger asked as he stared at them.

'The golden ones,' Macgillycuddy said. 'That is their village.'

And golden ones they are too, Badger thought, as they drew nearer. The children all wore short white robes. On their heads they wore thin gold bands. Both the boys' and the girls' hair was shoulder length and the most remarkable thing about them was their golden skin. Badger smiled at the happiness which surrounded him. Then the tallest of the children spoke.

'Welcome to our village, Grey One. My name is Cean. I am the head villager. You have come to save us and we are grateful. Come, and we will all eat on the green.'

Beano barked happily as some of the golden ones fussed around him. They avoided Macgillycuddy who scowled at them.

As Cean led Badger, Beano and the leprechaun through the village of tiny whitewashed cottages with thatched roofs and lovely flower filled gardens, they were followed by the children. Lions, tigers, antelopes and tiny does seemed to smile at them as they passed.

Beano and Badger gaped as a huge white lion walked around a corner with several tiny birds nesting in its thick furry collar. A leopard and a chicken, both white in colour, walked side by side past them. This is a beautiful place, thought Badger.

At last they reached the village green which was situated in a circle of twelve cottages. A curved rainbow danced above, its colours changing and rippling back and forth. In the centre of the green, Cean waited until all the villagers arrived. Then magically, chairs and tables laden with food appeared. Badger found himself sitting between Cean and another villager called Celan. Celan was almost the same height as Badger.

'I know you must be hungry, Grey One. You will eat heartily for you need to be strong for your first task.'

Badger turned to Celan who had spoken, then looked at Macgillycuddy.

'What is this about a first task?' he asked picking up a piece of mouth-watering meat. He bit into it thinking of his hunger, then Macgillycuddy answered his question.

'Oh yes, I forgot to tell you,' Macgillycuddy said through a mouthful of food. 'You have some tasks to perform. Five. I think . . . or is it four? No, it's five . . . or six . . . yes six . . . I think. Oh well, we'll find out soon enough.'

Badger glared at him. The little man was beginning to irritate him. Sitting just below Macgillycuddy under the table, Beano thought, as he tore at the most delicious piece of meat he had ever tasted, 'Master, something tells me the little man is not telling us everything.'

'Yes,' Badger thought. 'But I've a notion we'll soon find out about these tasks.'

As they ate, Beano and Macgillycuddy listened as Cean told Badger about their stolen golden rabbit.

'For thousands of years, it has brought our villages good fortune. But the evil ones came and stole it and placed it in the glen of the sithes.'

'Sithes?' Badger questioned.

'The banshees,' Macgillycuddy answered, lifting a glass of red wine.

'Nothing could harm us when we had our golden rabbit, but now . . . now . . .' Badger saw Cean's face grow sad.

'Now?' he asked.

'Now when the flowers sleep they come. . . .'

'They? Who?'

'The Harpies. . . .'

As he said 'Harpies' everyone at the table stopped eating and looked at him with fear in their eyes.

'You'll meet the Harpies soon, Grey One,' Macgillycuddy said, wiping his mouth with the tail of his bushy beard. Then he pushed his chair away from the table. 'They're women, you know,' he added. 'Ugly hags, with huge wings and sharp birdlike claws. You'll have to face them shortly. You and Beano. They will come soon to take a villager . . . or two.'

Badger stared at the little man aware that everyone was watching him.

'But why can't you all band together and drive these . . . these Harpies away. I'm sure all of you could beat them.'

'Pish pshaw,' Macgillycuddy said, picking a hair from his nose. 'You see, Grey One, the Harpies only come when all the villagers sleep. . . .'

Cean interrupted him saying, 'We have to sleep when the flowers sleep. We cannot stay awake even if we wanted to. The Harpies come and take one of us away each time. Soon,' he whispered, 'all of us will be gone.'

Badger looked around the table. All the villagers were nodding at him.

'Already I feel sleepy,' Celan added, his blue eyes creasing into a worried frown.

As Badger picked at the rest of his meal, he could feel the fear of the beautiful golden children increasing. Then a girl at the far end of the table yawned and beside her another girl suddenly slumped forward and was fast asleep.

'It is time. The flowers sleep,' whispered Celan.

Astonished, Badger watched as one by one the villagers fell asleep. With their heads lying on their plates they snored peacefully. At the edge of the green Badger could see that the animals were sleeping too. Just before Cean fell asleep he whispered, 'You've got to save us, Grey One. Only you can save. . . .'

Then Badger saw him lay his head on his hands and fall instantly asleep.

Beano came out from under the table.

'How long do they sleep for?' he asked Macgillycuddy.

'For as long as the flowers sleep.'

'How long is that?' Beano growled.

'Pish pshaw. How would I know?' the leprechaun snapped.

'You seem to know everything else!' Beano shouted.

'Be quiet, Beano!' Badger snapped. 'These Harpies . . . when do they come. . . .?'

Even as he spoke he knew that the Harpies were near. The belt of the Ancients was vibrating hard. Then he felt the magic course up through him and an idea came to him.

'Quick! Pretend to be sleeping. We must catch the Harpies unawares, but heaven knows how we are going to defeat them. Now don't speak at all when they get here. . . .'

'Master,' thought Beano, 'they're here already.'

The hair on Badger's head stood straight up as he heard the horrible screeching. With his head in his hands he pretended to sleep. Peeping out of one eye he could see that Macgillycuddy was lying with his cap over his eyes. When he saw the three creatures land on the green he couldn't stop shivering.

The Harpies were three metres tall with a wing span of at least seven metres. They had toothless, wrinkled, pale old women's faces and long greasy hair. They wore black cloaks that covered their twisted bodies. Their feet were like birds' feet with sharp claws fifty centimetres long. The spidery wings that grew from their hunched shoulders flapped vigorously as they moved towards one of the tables.

'Ha, ha, ha, ha. Fine pickings today, sisters,' one of them croaked. Smacking her lips she lifted a beautiful girl's hand and dropped it again. 'We'll feed well today . . . Wait! . . .'

Badger could feel his magic belt vibrate as the Harpy screamed, 'There are strangers here. They're not sleeping. Danger . . . sisters . . . Flee . . . Flee . . .'

With a single jump, Badger landed on top of the table, and Macgillycuddy and Beano joined him.

'Your reign of terror is over. You will never harm the villagers or anyone again!' shouted Badger.

'Flee . . . Flee. It is the Grey One . . . He has the magic to destroy us . . . Flee my sisters . . . Flee . . .'

Flapping their wings the screeching Harpies lifted high into the air but it was too late. Three beams of magical force hit them. Screaming with pain as a wing from each of them was singed to a stump, they flew erratically around. As more beams hit them, their three remaining wings disappeared. With loud thuds they landed on the green. Screaming through their toothless mouths with a mixture of pain and anger they raced towards Badger, their claws extended, ready to tear him apart.

A tiny beam shot from Badger's finger and hit Beano just on the point of his head. In a second he was thirty metres tall. With one paw he flattened the attacking Harpies. Badger and Macgillycuddy smiled as they saw Beano's head change to that of a giant cat. Then one by one, he tore the claws from the Harpies' feet, and spat them into the river beyond. Seconds later he shrank back to normal size when he saw that the Harpies were helpless. Sobbing, they hobbled away, their reign of terror over.

Later, when the villagers awoke again, Macgillycuddy told them what had happened. When the tears of joy had dried, Cean said, 'We must have a celebration, Grey One. You will stay and be honoured. . . .'

'No!' Macgillycuddy shouted. 'We have to get on. We must get across the river to the valley of the Horn.'

'Master,' Beano thought. 'this little man is beginning to annoy me. He knows more than he is letting on.'

'Yes, he does, doesn't he?' thought Badger.

One hour later, they left the village of the golden children and headed back towards the edge of the river Faughan.

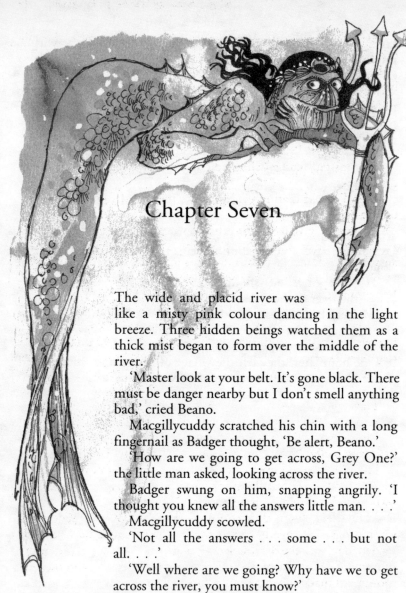

Chapter Seven

The wide and placid river was
like a misty pink colour dancing in the light
breeze. Three hidden beings watched them as a
thick mist began to form over the middle of the
river.

'Master look at your belt. It's gone black. There
must be danger nearby but I don't smell anything
bad,' cried Beano.

Macgillycuddy scratched his chin with a long
fingernail as Badger thought, 'Be alert, Beano.'

'How are we going to get across, Grey One?'
the little man asked, looking across the river.

Badger swung on him, snapping angrily. 'I
thought you knew all the answers little man. . . .'

Macgillycuddy scowled.

'Not all the answers . . . some . . . but not
all. . . .'

'Well where are we going? Why have we to get
across the river, you must know?'

'That is the thing, Grey One. I don't know. Your destiny is
mapped out for you . . . and the valley of the Horn is where we
have to go next, it lies in those mountains there.'

Badger looked in the direction he was pointing. The mountain
seemed to be beckoning them.

Just as Macgillycuddy was about to say something else, they all heard singing.

Floating around the corner, they saw a bearded old man pushing easily on a long handled oar which was fixed to the back of his sturdy looking raft.

He was singing,
'THE RIVER IS MY HOME, AND I AM AN OLD MAN
THE RIVER IS MY HOME, AND I SAIL WHERE I CAN.'

'Hey mister!' Badger shouted cupping his hands in front of his mouth.

'Eh?' The old man looked towards them and stopped pushing on the oar.

'Could you give us a lift to the far side? Please!'

The old man stared at them for a few moments, then he answered, 'I don't carry passengers,' and he began to row on.

'We need to get to the valley of the Horn it's very urgent', Badger pleaded.

The old man stopped.

'Need?' he shouted. 'What is need?' Moving closer and squinting over his bi-focals, he asked, 'Who are you who wants to get to that terrible place?'

'He is the Grey One!' Macgillycuddy yelled. 'You have to help him.'

'Have! . . . Have! . . .' the old man shouted angrily, beginning to row furiously. 'No one tells me what to do.'

'Please . . . please wait!' Badger shouted. 'We do need your help very badly. Please don't be angry . . . Won't you help us?'

The old man stopped rowing. 'I was captain once on a great four masted vessel but the pirates took it. This is the only craft I own now. You are not pirates, are you?'

As he drew closer, they could see that the raft was made from several logs tied together with thick hemp. At the back, a long bladed oar was fixed to a wooden pivot. The back and forth movement of the oar caused the raft to move forward, and the side movement made the raft change direction.

The old man was dressed in a naval captain's uniform. Under one arm he carried a shiny brass telescope. On his head he wore a captain's hat with the words 'S.S. TITANIC' written across it.

Beano began to bark. Turning, Badger was surprised to see Celan running towards them. 'Cean sent me to accompany you,

Grey One. He said I was to help you to bring our golden rabbit back to our village.'

'Master,' the thought came quickly from Beano. 'Look at your belt. The diamond has gone even blacker. Great evil is very near.'

Badger didn't have to look at the belt, for he could feel the magic surging into him. Now the words of the mushroom came to him as he looked at Celan. 'BEWARE OF FRIENDS. TRUST NO ONE BUT MACGILLYCUDDY AND YOUR FAMILIAR.' 'Aye master, the mushroom was right,' thought Beano.

Looking at Celan again, Badger reached out his hand saying, 'Thank you Celan. I'm sure you will be a great help to us.' Then he turned to the captain.

'Captain, would you be kind enough to take me and my friends across to the far side. We can't pay. . . .'

'Pay!' The old man's eyes flashed angrily for a moment, then broke into a soft smile. 'No need for that, young 'un. I was going that way myself. I'll be glad to give you a lift. Here boy!' he shouted, handing Celan the rope attached to the raft. 'You hold her near the bank and the rest of you can jump aboard.'

Beano jumped first, followed by Macgillycuddy who almost didn't make it. As he landed on the edge of the raft he lost his balance, and would have fallen into the river only for Beano who grabbed his belt with his sharp teeth and hauled him aboard. Then Badger leapt on board and as the raft moved out a bit, Celan sprang aboard too.

The captain took the oar and began to push on it. Beano sat between him and Celan, and Badger and Macgillycuddy sat near the front.

Badger could still feel the magic pumping into him, getting him ready. But ready for what? he thought. Beano stared towards the mist feeling very nervous and apprehensive.

'Right then, away we go!' shouted the captain, pushing on the oar a few times. Then he turned to Celan.

'Here lad, push on this. I'll keep a look out for pirates.' As Celan began to row there was a broad smile on his handsome gold face.

Beano stiffened as the captain walked past him to the edge of the raft. Something is not right, he thought. He turned to look up at Celan who was still rowing, sweat bubbling on his golden brow. Then with a deep sniff Beano smelled Celan's feet. No, he thought, there's no evil there.

'What's up, Beano?' The thought came from Badger.

'I don't know, master. Hold on.'

Rising again, Beano sniffed at the captain's feet while he was looking through his telescope. 'It's him!' he thought.

'Who, Beano?' Badger thought. 'Who?'

'It's the captain, master!' Beano shouted out loud. 'It's not Celan. The captain is a Mefisto. . . .'

From the vast deep it came, rising, rising, rising. Its ancient yawning mouth roaring its anger as it broke the surface. As the monster rose up out of the water, the captain swung around, his eyes flashing wickedly. With a curse he flung his telescope at Badger. Like lightning, Badger caught it and threw it back, hitting the evil Mefisto on the head as he turned to dive into the water.

'Fools . . . fools! . . .' he screamed, as he leapt into the churning water and disappeared in a puff of smoke.

Now they all stood to face the terrible creature from the bottom of the river. Roaring horribly it towered over the tossing raft. Macgillycuddy and Celan shook with terror as they held onto the oar to try to keep from falling in.

'Master, look out!' shouted Beano.

With its mouth gaping open, and its long scaly green neck writhing, the monster attacked. Badger leapt out onto the water with a terrified look on his face as the monster hit the raft and tipped the others into the river. Surrounded by a blue misty globe of magic, Badger ran towards the monster and with a flying leap he landed on its thorny head. Gripping the thick slimy skin he made two fierce barrages of raw magic burst from his hands into the creature's brain. Screaming in agony it dived below the surface, its spiked tail hitting the raft and smashing it to smithereens.

Still holding onto its head, Badger felt the monster plunge deeper and deeper. It was so dark that he didn't know whether he was going up or down. His magic still tore into the monster's brain until it stopped moving. Then Badger let go for he could see now that the monster was dead as it sank down to the depths of the bottomless river. It was only when it disappeared that he realised he could breathe underwater, and it was then he saw his first merman.

From the seaweed, ferocious-looking creatures appeared. The upper part of their scaly bodies looked like men with tiny gills on the side of their muscular necks. Their tails were twice as long as their bodies. They had no eyelids and they stared at Badger as they surrounded him. All the mermen carried three-pronged tridents.

Badger's heart pounded with fear as he saw them come nearer. I am finished, he thought, feeling for the belt. It was not vibrating. Why? he asked himself. Then the leader of the mermen spoke, answering his question. 'We do not wish to harm you, Grey One.' He smiled.

The merman who had spoken wore a gold, spiked crown.

Badger stared at him.

'Let me introduce myself. I am Norman, King of the mermen. I would like to thank you on behalf of my subjects.'

'Thank me?' stammered Badger, at the same time realising he could also speak underwater.

'Because you have rid our domain of the terrible Grack.'

'Grack?'

'Yes, it has terrorised our domain for some time. Now that it is dead, we can be happy again. You see it was the Evil One who put the Grack in our domain.'

'Mefistofelees?' Badger asked, noticing the king's face change as he heard the name.

'Yes, and now we would like to offer you our help. You and your companions.'

'Oh dear,' Badger exclaimed. 'I forgot about them. They are up above . . . in the water. . . .'

Turning ,the king nodded, and immediately ten mermen swam speedily towards the surface.

'They will see that your companions are safe.'

'I must get to the surface too,' Badger said.

'I will take you, hold my hand,' smiled the king.

A minute later, Badger, Beano, Macgillycuddy and Celan were bobbing about in the warm water surrounded by smiling mermen.

'Pish pshaw!' grumbled Macgillycuddy. 'Can you not get us out of this, Grey One? I hate water.'

Badger laughed, then spoke to the king.

'Do you think you could help us to get over to the other side of the river? We have to get to the valley of the Horn.'

'Why?' the king asked.

Badger turned to Macgillycuddy, who shrugged his shoulders as best as he could in the water.

'I don't know. We have to get there, that's all I know,' said Badger.

The king stared at the little man, then thought for a few moments. With a silent command he ordered fifty of the mermen to lie flat on the water facing downwards with arms linked, forming their bodies into a raft.

'Now Grey One. You and your companions get on board. We will transport you across.'

Seconds later, they were speedily heading for the far bank.

The mist had lifted, and the three beings who had been watching them had gone.

When they reached the bank, Badger and the others scrambled onto the land, and watched as the mermen unlinked themselves.

'Thank you,' Badger smiled, as the king pointed with his trident into the water. With great leaps the mermen soared into the air and with tiny splashes vanished below. Just before the king followed them he shouted, 'Remember, Grey One, if you ever need help again, my subjects and I will be here. We are forever grateful to you.' Then with a wave he flicked his tail and soared high into the air above the water, disappearing below without even as much as a tiny splash.

'Well what did you think of that, Beano?' Badger thought.

'Very exciting, master. It seems that something always turns up to help us.'

'Not something, Beano. Magic.'

Then Macgillycuddy spoke, pointing to the mountains ahead. 'Yonder is your first task.'

'First task?' Badger said loudly. 'What do you mean my first task? We have fought the Harpies, and the Mefistoes . . . and the Grack. . . .'

'Pish pshaw. Sure they weren't tasks, Grey One. Tasks are . . Well let me see. Your first task will be in the valley where there is a golden horn. You must find it. It will help you when you face other evils.'

'A horn? A golden horn? How can that help me?' Badger asked.

'How do I know. Pish pshaw, Grey One. You will need to have your wits about you to defeat the Evil One. Why do you ask so many questions? There's no need for them. Things will happen. Things that you have no control over. So let us get to your first task, the horn.'

Beano looked up at his master and growled as he thought, 'That little man is definitely beginning to annoy me, master.'

'Me too, Beano. But as he says, things will happen.'

Chapter Eight

Following Macgillycuddy they moved inland through fields thick with flowers and bees. As they reached a rocky pass they came to two tall stone pillars standing five metres apart. Above the pillars was a wooden sign which seemed to be floating in the air. On the sign was written the words,

'YOU ARE NOW ENTERING THE VALLEY OF THE HORN. YOU DO SO AT YOUR OWN PERIL.'

Hidden in the long grass to the left of the pillars, lay twenty Mefistoes watching them. Chattering in an ancient Irish language only they could understand, they changed into a flock of black doves. Flying into the air they hovered above Badger and the others as they entered the valley of the Horn.

The valley lay between two high snowcapped mountains. On both sides of the wide grassy path that wound through it, tall trees grew. They were thicker and taller than any Badger had ever seen before. The thick red trunks were hollow, so that when the light wind whistled through them they gave out a mournful hum. Badger shivered and he noticed Celan looking all around. He too was afraid. Beano and Macgillycuddy were walking ahead. Back came the thought from Beano, 'Master . . . beware . . . I feel. . . .'

Just then a tree crashed to the ground, separating Badger and Celan from Beano and the leprechaun. The belt, forcing magic through Badger, turned black. Quickly, with a wave of his arm

45

Badger made the giant tree rise into the air, so that he could see what was happening to Beano and Macgillycuddy.

They were standing in the middle of the path, as if they were hypnotised. Horrified, Badger and Celan could see that the black doves were drawing closer. Their wings were stiff and sharp as they whizzed towards the helpless leprechaun and dog.

Still holding the giant tree in the air, Badger shouted, 'Beano! Get out of there!'

'Master I can't,' thought Beano, his black eyes wide with fear as the sharp wings came nearer.

Suddenly, before Badger could think what to do, Celan ran forward. From a bag hung around his waist he took out another tiny bag and threw it at the doves. Instantly the powder that burst from the bag turned into a flock of hawks. Immediately they attacked the black doves. With cries of terror they flew to the ground and changed back into Mefistoes. Then they ran for safety into the trees still fighting off the fierce hawks.

'Get back here, now, Beano!' shouted Badger.

As Macgillycuddy and Beano ran to him he said, 'That is a lesson well learned. From now on we stick together. The Mefistoes will try again.'

'Pish pshaw, sure haven't I been telling you that all the time,' snapped Macgillycuddy.

'You haven't told us very much, Mac,' Badger said, glaring at him. 'It would be nice to know where we are going and when the tasks finish.'

The leprechaun looked up at him and his words made Badger feel afraid.

'The tasks will finish when you are strong enough to face Mefistofelees. Only then. That will be the final task. To over-come and destroy the Evil One . . . or . . . ,' he looked steadily at Badger, 'die. . . .'

Badger gulped.

'Don't listen to him, master,' Beano thought brightly. 'We've come this far. What more could happen to us? We're strong now, you and me. Nothing can defeat us.'

'I hope you're right Beano,' thought Badger, though he still felt afraid.

'We have to be getting on, Grey One,' Macgillycuddy said. 'The cave is just a mile around the next corner.' Then he began to walk on.

'Cave? What Cave? Mac, what are you talking about? Macgillycuddy! Answer me . . . Macgillycuddy. . . .' But the leprechaun paid Badger no heed and hurried along the path.

'Master, I'm hungry,' thought Beano.

'Me too,' sighed Badger as he felt his stomach rumbling. 'I shouldn't be hungry, it isn't that long since we ate at Celan's village.'

As they came around the corner, they all saw her at the same time. A woman sitting on a blanket in a little grove in the bushes. Beside her lay a basket of the biggest strawberries they had ever seen. The woman wore a white cloak with a hood which covered most of her face. All Badger could see of her face was a milky white skin and a firm round chin.

'Would you care to partake of some strawberries, young man?' the woman asked, in a voice that was strangely familiar to Badger. Instinctively he felt for the belt. It wasn't vibrating. He looked down at the diamond. It wasn't glowing.

'What do you think, Beano?' he thought.

'I don't sense any danger, master, and your belt isn't glowing black either. It has always warned us before . . . and master . . .'

'What?'

'Those strawberries look delicious.' Beano's tongue was hanging out and saliva was dripping from his mouth.

'Yes they do, don't they?' Badger thought, licking his lips.

'Then why don't you have some?' the woman asked offering him a strawberry the size of an apple.

As she handed Badger the fruit, her cloak moved back from her face and the light flashed from her even white teeth.

'I'd really like one . . . or two, but we don't have any money to pay you . . . at least . . . I . . .' He looked at Macgillycuddy and Celan.

'The strawberries are free, young man,' the woman smiled. 'It is an honour to feed the saviour of our land.' With another smile she stretched her hand further towards him. Badger hesitated, but not Beano who went right up to the woman's basket. She reached inside and placed some on the grass for him.

'Mmm master, these are delicious . . . mmmmmmm.'

'Thank you Miss . . . er . . . thank you,' Badger stammered, then took a bite. Soon all four were sitting beside the woman eating. Macgillycuddy smiled as he saw the woman hand Badger an extra one. He failed to see the Mefistoes watching them from the bushes, angry scowls on their faces.

'Where do you live?' Badger asked, taking a small bite from another strawberry.

'Here,' the woman replied. 'Well everywhere.' She bent her head as Badger tried to see her face more clearly.

Her voice, he thought. There's something strangely familiar about her voice. I feel I've heard it before.

The woman smiled as if reading his thoughts.

Then Beano sprang to his feet. Wagging his tail happily he thought, 'I'm ready for anything now, master. I feel fantastic.'

Badger smiled at him. Then the woman rose. 'I have to be going now, young man. Thank you for letting me be of service to you.'

'Thank you,' Badger said, 'but I don't even know your name.'

'My name? My name is Kathleen.'

'Why that was my mother's name,' Badger said staring at her.

'Yes,' answered the woman, bending and lifting her basket. 'Well goodbye, young man, and thank you again.'

With the basket in the crook of her arm she walked down the path that Badger and the rest had come up. Badger stared after her. Strange, he thought. Then as she rounded the corner and was out of sight, Macgillycuddy jumped to his feet.

'It's time we were going. We have to get to the cave.'

'The horn . . . yes . . .' sighed Badger, still looking in the direction the strange woman had gone.

As the four set off again, Badger thought about her.

'She was very nice, master,' said Beano.

'Yes Beano, she was. But I feel so sad. I wonder why?'

Meanwhile, the Mefistoes who had been watching them had doubled back and now they lay in wait for the woman.

As she passed by a group of coloured trees they suddenly sprang out and blocked the path in front of her. Their daggers were drawn.

The ugliest of them, who had two horns growing out of his brow, snarled, 'You have helped the Grey One, for that you must die.'

The rest of the Mefistoes advanced towards her, leering.

Slowly, the tall woman eased back the hood exposing her face. All the Mefistoes gasped, and staggered back from her. From a point in the middle of her forehead, to the back of her head, a five centimetre band of white hair grew, widening as it spread into her

waist length hair. Her brown eyes began to glow and the Mefistoes were bathed in the brown light that emanated from them.

Ten seconds later she walked around them and continued on her way. The Mefistoes stared in a trance, unable to move. Only when the woman was out of sight were they able to come round. Then chattering angrily they headed into the bushes.

Chapter Nine

'Is that the cave?' Badger asked, his voice shaky as he stared up at the black entrance into the hill.

'What do you think?' Macgillycuddy said, looking at the cave too.

Badger sighed, scrambling up the rocks while Beano and the others followed him. As he looked down into the dark foreboding cave, Badger whispered, 'How will we see the horn, Mac? It's very dark in there.'

'You will see it alright, Grey One. It lies on a diamond table.'

'A diamond table!' Badger exclaimed staring at the little man.

'Aye, a large black diamond table.'

Badger studied Macgillycuddy's inscrutable face and said, 'So all I have to do, is go into that cave and take the horn from the top of the diamond table?' Already he could feel the belt vibrating and knew it wasn't going to be that easy.

'I didn't say that, Grey One,' Macgillycuddy whispered. His face had gone a deathly white as he added, 'There are . . . things . . . down there. . . .'

'Things?' Badger shuddered. 'What do you mean, things?'

'Things . . . I don't know . . . but many have tried to get the horn. Many have entered the cave and none have returned.'

'And you want me to go in there?' Badger said aghast.

'You and your Familiar. . . .'

'Look little man,' Beano growled, sliding beside his master, 'I told you I don't like being called a Familiar. Dog will do, if you can't call me by my name. . . .'

'Beano,' thought Badger, 'Be quiet. We have to think this out. Can you see the belt. It's glowing and the magic is building up inside me. I've never felt it so strong.'

Beano looked at the diamond buckle and he could feel the force of the terrible things that dwelled in the cave. 'Master,' he thought, 'I don't feel too happy about going in there.'

'Neither do I! But it appears we have to. At least I feel we have to.'

Then turning to Macgillycuddy he asked, 'This horn. What's so special about it?'

'It was placed there by the Ancients. Long, long ago. You are to recover the horn from its guardians, blow it and then return here with it and your first task is over. But enough of this, Grey One. You will know what to do when you are inside. It's time. . . .'

Badger shivered, then reluctantly, with Beano close beside him, he scrambled down into the darkness.

They had only gone a few metres when suddenly, in glowing crystals above them, the words BEWARE ALL WHO DARE ENTER THE CAVE OF THE HORN appeared. Gulping, Badger felt more magic pump into him.

Five minutes later he thought, 'Beano, can you see anything?'

'No, but I can feel much evil, and it's very near,' came the reply.

As Badger stepped along the hard stony floor, his foot hit a piece of rock and it rolled on down into the darkness. As the rumbling noise from the rolling rock grew louder and louder they knew that whatever was in the cave had been warned.

'SSSSSS . . . ARRRGGHHHHHH . . .' the terrible roar that followed made the white hairs on both the boy and the dog stand straight up. Gulping with fear, Badger thought, 'Did you hear that?'

'Yes, master,' Beano thought back, and Badger detected the dreadful fear in him.

Suddenly, magical light beamed from Badger's eyes, and he walked on. Beano followed looking all around. Now they moved deeper into the cave until it widened out into a huge cavern. In the middle of the floor lay the horn on a huge diamond. High above in the stalactities that hung from the roof, five things roared simultaneously and then began to drop onto the cavern floor with loud thuds.

Gasping with fresh-creeping horror, Badger and Beano saw three of the things slither towards them.

The things were thirty metres long with slimy snake bodies as broad as a horse's back. The most horrible thing about them was their heads, they looked like bearded men, with long forked, poisonous tongues which flicked in and out between their curved canine teeth. Their huge round, bulging eyes blazed with horrible intent. Each of the things had four muscular arms and instead of hands had claws like a giant lobster, which opened and snapped shut as they crawled nearer. Horrified, Badger saw that they were slithering over the skeletons of the many others who had entered their lair.

'SSSSS . . . ARRRGGHHHHHHH. . . .'

'Master, move!' shouted Beano, as he saw his master was trans-fixed with fear. But he needn't have worried, for just as the nearest thing lunged at Badger with its fiercesome claws snapping, Badger leapt into the air above its head. Quickly he snapped his fingers twice. Screaming in terrible pain the thing slithered away as both its eyes exploded. Now the other two rose up to try and reach Badger.

When Beano saw that the two things were more interested in his master, he ran towards the table. It glowed as he came nearer, warning the horrible creatures. One of them dived at him with lightning speed. But Beano, surrounded by a purple glow of magic, became twice as fast and easily leapt out of the way. Screaming with anger the two things tried to grab him, but faster than a shooting star, Beano easily avoided their terrible claws.

While Beano was keeping the two things that attacked him at bay, Badger had become a round glowing orb of magic. Moving back and forwards he began to hypnotise the brutes. Their horrible eyes grew glazed and slowly their hissing roars died away and they began to sway. In seconds they were making soft snoring noises. Badger lowered himself to the ground, satisfied they were asleep. Then he turned to see how Beano was coping.

'Master, I can't keep this up forever. What's keeping you?' Beano thought.

'Let me think, Beano. Ah, now I know.'

Walking closer to the things attacking Beano, Badger waved his hands. Several thick beams of magic burst towards their tails. Beano woofed happily as he saw that the slimy bodies were beginning to tie themselves in knots. Then before they knew it, the horrible crea-tures were helpless. With another burst of magic Badger shot them to the far side of the cavern where the other blind thing squirmed.

'Hurry and get the horn, master,' Beano thought, looking at the hypnotised things. 'They're beginning to wake up.'

Going right up to the glowing diamond table, Badger reached for the golden horn. It was about the size of his hand, and as he lifted the horn the table turned completely black, and began to sink into the ground. On the roof of the cavern the stalactites wobbled, and some began to fall.

'Quick Beano!' Badger shouted as he pulled the chain attached to the horn onto his shoulder. 'Let's get out of here!'

Badger and Beano ran to the exit.

As they left the cavern, all the stalactites fell and the horrible creature's shrieks died quickly away as the rest of the cavern roof fell in.

When they came running out from the cave, Macgillycuddy and Celan cheered. Then Macgillycuddy shouted, 'Blow the horn, Grey One. Blow it!'

Putting the horn to his lips Badger blew and the weird sound echoed along the valley.

Mefistofelees cursed as the sound reached him.

'So!' he roared, 'the chosen boy has won the accursed horn. Well it won't do him much good.'

The two horns on his head glowed with an evil aura as he spat flame at two hunchbacked little men who were stoking the giant fire with the bodies of the evil dead.

When the echoes had died away, Badger looked at Macgillycuddy. As if reading his mind the little man pointed to a winding path at the far end of the valley.

'We must head for there. That path leads up to yonder mountain.'

High above, Badger could see the mountain, a ring of mist shrouding its pointed peak.

'What is there?' he asked, afraid to know the answer.

Macgillycuddy reached inside his badgerskin long john, and withdrew a tiny leather flask. Opening it he took a drink. Smacking his lips he then wiped them with the end of his bushy beard.

'You have to read the Ancient words,' he said, replacing his flask.

'I must what?' Badger asked, as Macgillycuddy headed off in the direction of the path. Quickly he followed him asking for an explanation on the way.

'There is a parchment with Ancient words written on it. Only you can read them. The written words lie in the middle of a block of ice up in yonder mountain. You have to enter the place where the creature who guards it lives. You must read the words, and be able to understand them. Don't ask me why you have to do this, but I suspect it will help when you face HIM.'

As they walked on Badger stared at the leprechaun, then he asked, 'How come, you know all this, Mac? Why can't you tell me about the other tasks? How many more tasks are after this one?'

'Two more . . . or is it three . . . No two . . . definitely two . . . I think . . . I can't seem to remember,' Macgillycuddy replied, a sly glint in his eyes. 'But it will come to me. Don't worry, Grey One . . . It will come to me.'

Badger turned and raised his eyes to Celan, who grinned.

Then Beano thought, 'That little squirt is really getting on my nerves, master. But you know, I'm really looking forward to the tasks.'

Badger smiled, 'So am I, but I'm not looking forward to meeting Mefistofelees.'

Chapter Ten

The path leading up to the mountain skirted around the edge of a lough. As they walked around it Beano growled as he felt the evil presence.

'Yes, Beano,' Badger thought, 'I feel it too. Stay alert.'

Leading the way was Macgillycuddy, while Celan walked behind Badger and Beano. His piercing blue eyes searched the rocks at the bottom of the mountain. He too felt afraid.

As he looked towards the start of the path that would take them up the mountain, he failed to see a thick, slimy tentacle slip from the still water of the lough. Silently it encircled his legs. Before he knew it he was held fast and was being pulled towards the water.

'Help!' he cried, as he struggled to free himself. Now more tentacles splashed from the lough and before Badger could think, a hundred tentacles had wrapped themselves all around them and were dragging them into the water.

Badger shot a burst of magic at the water. A tentacle had sucked itself around his head covering his eye. Immediately, the water froze solid. At the same time the tentacles stopped moving and grew limp. Quickly the four freed themselves. Their relief at being free was short lived, for screeching in a terrifying voice, the monster, which Macgillycuddy later told them was called a Decipus, because it had one hundred tentacles, burst through the ice and began ripping its tentacles free.

They all gasped as they stared at the Decipus. Its one eye was two hundred centimetres round, and its terrible crunching maw opened and closed. Inside its maw, they could see its black jagged teeth grinding with anger. Then it began to move towards them, its sucking tentacles flicking at them like giant whips.

'Quick, get behind the rocks!' shouted Badger. 'I'll handle it.'

'But master,' Beano thought.

'Beano, do as you're told,' Badger screamed as he faced the Decipus. He waited, standing still, as its tentacles whipped around him. Then, just as the creature got ready to pull him into its open maw, Badger turned red hot. The others gasped as they saw him change into a burning boy of molten metal. Screaming in agony the Decipus released him. Now Beano and the others watched in horror as they saw Badger suddenly spring straight into the monster's gaping maw.

'He's gone,' Beano thought, 'My master is gone.'

'No I'm not. Stop worrying, Beano. I'm O.K. Watch this.'

Startled, Macgillycuddy, Beano and Celan saw the Decipus lift into the air. Up, up, up it floated until it was almost out of sight, hovering for a few seconds before it plummeted towards the lough. It hit the water with a mighty smack, splashing every drop out of it. Drenched, Beano and the others stared into the hole where the lough had been, and saw the many bones of others who had been taken by the Decipus. Macgillycuddy looked for Badger, wondering where he was, then he felt a hand on his shoulder.

'Aren't you going to lead the way, Mac?' Badger asked, a smile on his face. Beano barked happily.

'You had us worried, master,' he thought.

Then with another look at the floundering, dazed Decipus they continued on their way.

Halfway up the mountain, the three beings watched from the cover of the mist. Then they floated on up the mountain.

Later, as they climbed, Badger questioned Macgillycuddy.

'How will we know when we are near the mountain creature's lair?'

'A Gorbear, Grey One. It's called a Gorbear,' the little man snapped.

'A Gorbear? What's that?'

'I would say it's a cross between a Gorilla and a bear . . . except . . .'

'Except?' Badger said, hating to hear what was coming next.

'Except it's fifty metres tall.'

Badger gasped, and Beano almost choked, 'Fifty metres tall . . . surely not. . . .'

Then Beano thought, 'Sure master, it's just a big bear of some sort. We can handle it . . . don't worry.'

'Who's worried?' Badger thought. 'I'm just terrified.' He smiled grimly as he picked up the laughing thoughts from Beano. He wondered what he would have done without him. He shivered. It was getting colder.

'Aye,' Macgillycuddy said looking at him. 'It is getting colder.'

A light snow shower had started growing heavier by the time they came to the pass.

'We'll never get across that,' stated Celan looking out over the edge. A mile below, jagged rocks stuck up like giant stalagmites.

'The way to the Gorbear's lair,' Macgillycuddy said, pointing.

In the distance they could see the entrance to the lair through a narrow opening neatly cut into the ice.

'But how are we going to get across?' Celan asked, looking once more down the precipice.

Badger thought for a few minutes as the belt thrilled him with magic. Then he said to Macgillycuddy, 'We can't all go across. You and Celan will have to stay here.'

Just as he finished speaking they all heard a loud roar which shook the heavy snow from the cliffs overhead.

'The Gorbear,' Macgillycuddy whispered, looking very scared. 'He knows you are here, Grey One.'

'Can I go with you, Grey One?' Celan asked. 'I haven't been much help to you. Perhaps I could be, over there.' He nodded across the pass, his handsome face glowing with the cold.

'No, Celan,' Badger replied. 'It is better if Beano and I go alone. We have the magic. It will be easier if we don't have to worry about you. I'm sorry. . . .'

'Yes, I understand,' Celan whispered, his face downcast.

'Pish pshaw! Are you going or not, Grey One? We are wasting time standing here,' Macgillycuddy snapped. 'I'm getting my death of cold.'

With a smile, Badger turned to Beano, then stepped straight off the precipice, his magic still surging through him. Celan gasped, but instead of Badger falling to his death, he seemed to be walking on an invisible bridge.

'C'mon Beano,' he shouted.

Barking happily, Beano followed him. Seconds later they were safely across. With a wave they turned and headed towards the ice on the way to the Gorbear's lair.

Chapter Eleven

'Easy Beano, I think it's along here . . .'

'How do you know, master?' Beano thought, shivering as he looked ahead into the dull, blue light.

'I know, come on.'

They soon came to a massive opening in the thick ice.

'Look at the size of that doorway, master,' Beano thought, his breath smoking in the cold air. Badger could feel the magic gush through him as Beano added, 'maybe we should go back.'

'Don't be silly, Beano. We couldn't go back now, even if we wanted to. Our magic wouldn't allow us. We have to go in. Come on.'

Badger could feel the nervousness of Beano's thoughts break into his own as they walked on into the Gorbear's lair, shivering with cold.

After five minutes of steady walking they began to feel warmer. At last they reached what they were looking for. A huge block of solid ice, clear as crystal and smooth as glass. The block was ten metres square, and in the very centre was the parchment with red writing on it. Words that Badger could not understand.

Ηαουτ   ϑΟΙΕ∗   Ιφοφωτ   ΓΛΟΩΕΟ

'I can't make out what they mean,' thought Badger, 'they look very strange.'

'You have to try, master, or all this will have been a waste of time. I don't like it here, I want to . . .'

Suddenly, they heard a loud roar which reverberated throughout the lair. Turning, they saw that the Gorbear was looking at them, standing on its hind legs. Silently it studied the terrified boy and his dog.

The Gorbear had the head of a hairy white gorilla, and two big ivory tusks curving outwards from its sharp teeth. The rest of its body was that of a giant white grizzly bear. But the thing that horrified them most was its height. Macgillycuddy had told them that it was fifty metres tall and that was hard enough to imagine. Now that the Gorbear was standing on its hind legs they could hardly see its terrible head. Suddenly the beast dropped on all fours and slowly closed on them. Saliva splashed from its mouth to the floor like tiny waterfalls.

'You must try and learn the words, master,' Beano thought quickly. 'I will keep the Gorbear occupied.'

A magical force swirled around him as the Gorbear raised its huge paw to strike. Then Badger saw that Beano was growing bigger and bigger until in seconds he was sixty metres tall. Badger smiled as he turned to look at the parchment. As he stared he saw the letters change position. It is definitely four words, he thought, but what do they mean?

Beano surprised the Gorbear by speaking to it in its own language.

'We have not come to harm you, oh great Gorbear. My master only wants to read the parchment. Then we will leave you in peace.'

'You can't read the parchment,' growled the Gorbear, quickly recovering from his surprise. 'It's not allowed.'

'And who doesn't allow it?' Beano asked, one eye watching his master walk around the block of ice.

'I don't know,' the Gorbear growled. 'I only know it's not allowed. I have to kill anyone who comes in here.'

'But we won't harm you. Look, you can keep the parchment. My master only wants to read the words, then we will go. You can still go on guarding it. . . . No one will know it's been read . . .'

'Well, I . . . I . . . don't know. . . .' the Gorbear stammered, looking confused.

'We will go, after my master has read it, and then you can guard it forever. No one would dare face you. You are the most magnificent creature I have ever seen.'

'Master,' Beano thought, as the Gorbear blushed even whiter, 'what's keeping you?'

'It's hard, Beano, very hard. I don't . . . Wait! . . . Wait! . . . Yes, I can understand what they say now . . . I understand the words.'

Smiling he looked up at the two animals towering above him.

'He's not very big, this master of yours,' the Gorbear said, looking down at Badger. More saliva hit the floor just in front of Badger, making him dive out of the way.

'He can get big if he wants to. Much bigger than you or I put together, but he is my master, and he would never harm me.'

The Gorbear looked down at Badger for a few moments, then asked, 'Do . . . do you think he would be my master, too?' Then he added, 'I get very lonely up here, all by myself.'

'Of course he can be your master. But we both have to go now. I mean, if that's all right with you? We can come and visit you another time.'

The Gorbear growled slowly as he looked at the giant Beano who winked at him. Then he looked down at Badger. Then at Beano, then down at Badger, then back at Beano again.

'Well, if you promise to come back and visit me, again,' he said sadly.

Beano smiled.

'Of course, Gorbear. I promise that we will visit this land a lot from now on, and we will certainly visit you, for you are my friend . . . and my master's friend too. Ahem . . . er . . . Can I get smaller again? That is, if it's all right with you? I get a bit light headed up here.'

'If you want to,' the Gorbear said, watching as Beano shrunk to his normal size.

'Is it O.K. Beano?' Badger thought, nodding up at the Gorbear who was watching them.

'Yes, master. I have made a promise on your behalf, that we will come and visit him again. He says he's very lonely up here.'

'Is he?'

'Yes.'

'Maybe I could do something about that.'

'How?'

'Watch!'

With a quick wave of his hands, Badger pointed at a wall of ice at the far end of the lair. Slowly, the ice began to melt and change into the shape of another Gorbear. Roaring with joy, the

Gorbear shuffled towards his new friend, delighted to have some-one to keep him company during the long winter.

As they watched the two Gorbears embrace, Badger said, 'I think it's time we were going, Beano.'

With a last look around at the happy Gorbears, Beano followed his master back to the pass.

At the far side of the pass Celan and Macgillycuddy were waiting for them. There was no sign of the Mefistoes, yet as Badger walked over the invisible bridge he could feel his belt vibrating.

'Master . . .'

'Yes, Beano . . . I know. Something evil is close.'

They stopped beside Celan and Macgillycuddy, ignoring the feeling of powerful magic. Badger asked Macgillycuddy, 'Well Mac, where to now?' He waited to see if the little man would ask him about the words. Badger intended to tease him, but Macgillycuddy scratched his head and said,

'Where to? . . . Why along here, then down again to the valley.'

'You never asked me about the parchment or if I understood the words!'

'Words?' Macgillycuddy said stupidly. Badger frowned and stared at him. The belt was vibrating disturbingly. Something was wrong. 'Beano, talk to Celan, ask him some questions,' he thought.

'Well Mac, what's the next task then?' he asked, as they slowly descended the mountain.

'Task? What do you mean?' the leprechaun asked. 'Oh yes, task. Well, you'll find out when we reach the bottom.'

As they walked through the thick mist they questioned Celan and Macgillycuddy. Beano too, could feel something was wrong, but he couldn't understand what it was.

'Master, Celan doesn't seem to be the same. Something is wrong with him. He . . . he smells different.'

'Yes Beano I know. Mac is behaving very strangely too, and the belt is really forcing the magic into me. It's preparing me for something. Keep alert.'

Just ahead in the mist the Mefistoes waited.

'Pish pshaw!' Macgillycuddy suddenly exclaimed, as they came to the mist. 'The heel of my boot is loose. You go on ahead, Grey One. I'll be along presently.'

Badger stared at the little man for a few moments, unable to keep still as the magic vibrated into him. As he turned to follow Beano and Celan into the mist, Macgillycuddy drew a dagger from inside his longjohn, and crept up behind Badger. Raising the dagger he was just about to plunge it into Badger's back, when a misty globe of blue magic burst from the back of Badger's head and encircled him. Screaming with pain, he dropped his dagger and changed back into the Mefisto that he really was. Swinging around, Badger saw the evil leprechaun's horns melting as he fell in agony on the ground.

'Beano,' Badger thought quickly, 'Celan has been turned into a Mefisto. Watch out. Get beside me quickly.'

In a flash Beano flew backwards from the mist and landed beside him. Celan and twenty other Mefistoes screamed out of the mist towards them. In seconds, Badger and Beano were surrounded by the evil little men.

'This time, Grey One, you will not survive,' the leader of the Mefistoes snarled, as he fingered the point of his dagger. Several Mefistoes carried heavy chains with spiked steel balls attached to them. These they whirled about, setting up a fearful noise. Seven other Mefistoes gripped thorn studded shillelaghs.

'What have you done with my friends?' Badger shouted, unafraid, as the magic sparkled around him and Beano.

'They are being well looked after, fool. But you need not concern yourself about their fate, for you will never see them again. . . .'

With that, the leader leapt forward cursing loudly, his dagger stabbing at Badger. In a flash Badger nodded slightly and a burst of sheer magic hit the Mefisto on the head. Startled and afraid, the other evil Mefistoes saw their leader twist in agony as his horns melted and his life's blood gushed over his ugly face which was gradually melting. He fell to the ground and disappeared.

The Mefistoes were staggered. From out of the mist a voice boomed.

'Attack! Attack! Kill them. All of you. They can't handle all of you. Attack! . . .'

'Who is that, master,' Beano thought, trying to see into the mist.

'Never mind about that now, Beano. Be prepared.'

As the screaming Mefistoes attacked them from all sides, there was only one way to go, and that was up. Just as the

Mefistoes reached them, Badger and Beano shot into the air. From twenty metres above the Mefistoes, magic burst from their eyes and hit the evil beings on their heads. In ten seconds half of them suffered the same fate as their leader. In a panic now, the others got ready to run.

'Change . . . fools! Change and destroy!' The voice from the mist boomed. 'Become birds . . . Change and destroy!'

As Badger and Beano hovered above the ground, they were horrified to see the remaining Mefistoes change into giant eagles. Screeching with anger they rose into the air. Their quick eyes burning red, the eagles swooped towards their quarry.

Suddenly, with a loud frizzle, Badger felt a bolt of magic shoot from him into Beano, transforming him into an eagle ten times bigger than his attackers.

With his huge wing span and his claws as long as a cricket bat Beano tore into the terrified eagle mefistoes. While Beano was chasing them all over the sky, Badger landed on the ground, only to find the real Celan and Macgillycuddy being guarded by three cloaked figures.

Silently the three cloaked Druids, for that's what they were, glared at him. Suddenly came a force so great that it caught Badger unawares, causing him to stagger backwards.

Macgillycuddy gasped as he saw what had happened. The Grey One is surely finished, he thought.

'The chosen one seems to be at a disadvantage, brothers,' chuckled one of the Druids. Silently all three raised their talon like hands. Badger felt himself bombarded with the powerful evil magic forcing him to the ground. The Druids came closer, their hands still pointing at him. For a second, Badger felt a sharp pain, but then magic even more powerful than the Druids surged through him, and he rose to his feet.

Macgillycuddy heaved a sigh of relief.

Behind their hoods, the Druids' eye sockets widened as they looked at Badger. The white hair on his head changed through all the colours of the rainbow, and from his piercing eyes burst such blasts of magical magnitude that it caused the three Druids to move back screaming. As Badger raised his hands to destroy them, they began to disappear from the feet up.

'We will meet again, Grey One. The next time you will not find it so easy. . . .' With that they vanished.

Almost at the same time, Beano returned and both boy and dog became normal once again.

'Your magic defeated the evil Druids, Grey One. It is powerful indeed.'

'The Druids? What is he talking about, master?' asked Beano, unaware of what had happened to Badger. 'Is this the real Macgillycuddy?'

'I'll explain later, Beano. A lot happened in the last few minutes.'

Later when all four were near the bottom of the path, Macgillycuddy inquired, 'I presume you read the words on the parchment?'

'Yes, Mac, but do you know, I can't seem to remember them no matter how hard I try.'

'Never mind, Grey One. They will come to you when you need them.'

'Will they?'

'Aye, be in no doubt about that,' Macgillycuddy said, his face growing pale. 'Let us get to the glen.'

'The glen?'

'Aye, the glen of the banshees.'

'What's a banshee?' Badger asked.

'You will know when you meet them,' Macgillycuddy answered mysteriously.

Celan spoke, his face looking grim.

'The glen is where the evil Mefistoes took our golden rabbit.'

Badger looked at him as Beano thought,

'Golden rabbit. I bet that's the next task, master.'

'Is getting the rabbit the next task, Mac?' asked Badger.

'Aye,' the little man said quickly, then hurried on.

Seeing that he was not going to get any more information from the leprechaun, Badger quizzed Celan.

'This glen, Celan, tell me about it.'

'It's a place to be avoided, Grey One. Some time ago a hundred of our villagers went there to try and take our rabbit back. Only one returned.'

'One?'

'Yes. The banshees let him go to warn the rest of us to keep out of their domain. You see, they think our golden rabbit is their God, but it isn't. It is our magic. Our village needs it.'

Badger frowned at the handsome Celan.

'Need it, why?'

'Pish pshaw,' Macgillycuddy interrupted angrily. 'Questions . . . questions. . . . So many questions. We'll never get to the glen before dark at this rate. Hurry, we have to hurry.'

Badger stopped and glared at him. Then Macgillycuddy shrugged his shoulders.

'The golden rabbit if you must know, is the key to the very existence of the village of the golden ones. It is their magic as Celan has said. Because it was not in its rightful place in the village, the Harpies were able to come. More terrible creatures will enter the village if the rabbit is not returned soon.'

'I see,' said Badger turning to look at the worried frown on Celan's face.

'Come now . . . keep up. . . . We must get to the glen before dark. . . . Keep up. . . .' shouted Macgillycuddy darting on.

Chapter Twelve

In silence they followed Macgillycuddy.

'Master, something evil is up ahead,' thought Beano silently.

'Mac, stop!' Badger shouted quickly. 'I hear something hissing . . . listen. . . .'

The little leprechaun tilted his head and listened with the others. Sure enough, they all heard the loud hissing sounds.

'Master, I'll go to the corner,' thought Beano.

'No, Beano. You stay here. I'll go with Mac and see what awaits us. The belt is at work already.'

Beano looked at the throbbing diamond and shivered. 'What next?' he thought.

'I don't know,' Badger thought back.

Celan and Beano watched as Badger and Macgillycuddy slowly rounded the corner. What they saw shocked them both.

Along the path were snakes of every description imaginable. The way was barred. Adders, vipers, cobras, huge anacondas, rattlesnakes rattling, diamond heads, boa constrictors were all crawling and wriggling and sinuously twisting. They were waiting for the travellers.

'How are we going to get to the glen through that lot?'

'Beano, you stay by my feet,' ordered Badger, 'Mac, you climb on Beano's back. Celan, you stand just behind me, and don't move.'

Without question the three did as they were told.

Already the shadows were lengthening down the valley.

'It's beginning to get dark,' Macgillycuddy whispered. 'It will be dark when we reach the glen of the banshees. That is, if we ever get there. . . .'

'We'll get there,' Badger said. With magic fizzling around him he reached out his left hand making circular movements creating a shimmering wall of magic to surround them. 'Let's go!' he shouted, smiling as he received Beano's fearful thoughts.

'We're not going to walk right through them master, are we?'

'We won't be harmed. The magic will protect us.'

And it did.

Beano could see that his master was right as they walked through the hissing snakes. He began to feel a lot happier but something worse was to come.

Badger was the first to see the Druids floating towards them.

'Stay where you are!' Badger shouted, rising quickly into the air to face the Druids and at the same time pointing his finger to make a wall of magic to protect his friends.

'It seems you are in a fine predicament, Grey One. You have to divide your power to keep the magic barrier in place, and use the rest to do battle with us. Will it be enough, Grey One? Somehow, we don't think so.'

With that, the Druids separated and hovering closer they surrounded Badger before he had time to think. His magic set to work. With one hand, he formed a protective ring around himself. Using his other hand, he changed the wall protecting the others into a ball of blue magic which began to roll through the snakes bringing them to safety.

Badger then began to spin faster and faster until millions of thin beams of magic burst from every part of his body and with loud crackles hit the Druids. Surprised by the sudden onslaught of good magic the Druids cloaks began to burn and they vanished with terrified roars screaming: 'We will be avenged for this, Grey One. We will see you suffer. We will return when you least expect us, and the next time you will be destroyed. . . .'

Ignoring their words, Badger floated over the snakes compelling the Blue Ball to roll faster and faster past the last of the snakes. Then with a loud electrical pop it burst and Celan, Beano, and Macgillycuddy rose to their feet.

'Close, Master. Very close,' Beano thought.

'Not really, Beano. I was in total control.'

'You are learning fast,' said Macgillycuddy. 'It's nearly dark. I had hoped we would be in the glen before dark.'

Beano stared at the scared little man. 'Master, I've never seen him look so scared before.'

Badger studied Macgillycuddy as they began to walk on. 'Neither have I, Beano.'

Shadows from the mountain covered the trees in the valley below and darkness fell.

They all shivered, and Badger's belt seemed to moan as it began to prepare him for what was to come next.

Chapter Thirteen

Twenty minutes later, they reached the trees in the valley. The eerie stillness was broken only by the hooting of an owl.

'That doesn't sound like an ordinary owl to me, master,' said Beano shivering.

'Which way in, Mac?' Badger asked, not answering him.

'Follow me,' Macgillycuddy whispered, 'and be very quiet. We don't want to disturb them. . . .'

'Them?'

'The banshees. . . .' the little man answered pushing further through the trees.

Silently they followed him.

'Master, I'm really scared.'

'Beano, stop it! The belt is going crackers. I need to concentrate.' Even as he spoke he could feel the build up of magical energy filling him with a deep awareness of his task.

'CRACK!' The sound of a twig breaking under Celan's foot echoed through the rustling trees. The owl hooted again, and they all stood still.

'Sorry,' whispered Celan, his pale gold face just visible.

Then they heard it. Softly at first. Like a wind whistling through the trees. It came in soft waves of eerie sound that kept up an incessant pitch as they stumbled through the darkness towards the light ahead.

'Easy,' Macgillycuddy whispered. 'I don't think they know we're here yet.'

Hardly daring to breathe, they crept closer to the light. Suddenly the wailing stopped.

'What now?' Badger asked, looking down at Macgillycuddy.

'I'm glad it has stopped, Master,' Beano's thoughts interrupted. 'The noise was getting unbearable, can you feel the evil?'

'Yes, Beano. A lot of evil, but I'm ready for it.'

Cautiously the four peered through the trees into the bright clearing. It was about the size of the inside of a cathedral. In the middle lay a very thick tree trunk where the golden rabbit sat, honoured by hundreds of staring banshees who were in a trance-like state.

The banshees were wraith-like, ghostly figures, and wore black hooded cloaks. Their grinning skull-like faces peeked from under their hoods as they began to wail softly again. Several of them bowed down before the golden rabbit, and all the time it glowed.

Below him in the undergrowth, Badger could feel Beano tremble with fear and he wondered why he wasn't feeling afraid. Gradually an idea came to him and he smiled as he thought about it.

Seconds later he whispered his plan to them.

'Can you do that, Beano?' asked Celan, looking in awe at the dog.

'Easy peasy, Celan,' woofed Beano quietly.

'Pish pshaw, it had better work. The sooner I am out of here the better. . . .' Macgillycuddy said gruffly.

'Right then, you three hide here. I'll draw the banshees off.'

Giving them the thumbs up sign, Badger bent low and began to slip through the trees. When he reached the clearing he stepped forward without hesitation.

'Hallo there!' he shouted cheekily. 'I've come for the golden rabbit.'

With loud wails of surprise the banshees gaped at him. 'It's the Grey One,' they all hissed, crowding around Badger and separating him from the golden rabbit.

Their leader stepped towards him, dressed in a dull, red cloak and reaching up she threw back her hood, exposing the long black hair growing out of her skull-like head.

Beano and the others gasped as they saw the rest of the banshees do likewise. Badger didn't have to pretend he was scared. He put his plan into action, letting out a loud shriek of fear, and ran back into the trees.

'After him, my sisters!' shouted the leader of the evil beings. 'Our Lord Mefistofelees will be pleased with us if we destroy the Grey One. After him!'

Floating across the clearing they pursued Badger, who had soared high into the trees.

Now, Beano thought, it's my turn.

Looking around them, Beano and Celan ran into the clearing to the golden rabbit. Stretching, Celan lifted it down.

'Go quickly!' Beano woofed, and floated up onto the tree trunk. Celan watched as Beano transformed himself into a golden rabbit.

'Go, I said!' Beano shouted. With a last look, Celan hurried back to the leprechaun, carrying the rabbit. He was just in time. Badger floated back onto the ground shouting, 'Here I am!' just as he stopped beside the tree trunk.

'O.K. Beano,' he thought. 'Get ready. They'll be here in a minute.'

Seconds later the wailing banshees, all of them with their heads still uncovered, dashed into the clearing.

'Fool!' the leader screamed floating towards him. 'Did you really think that you could steal our Great God rabbit? It seems your powers have been greatly exaggerated by the Mefistoes. You will not leave here alive . . . and neither will your Familiar and the others. . . . We know they are somewhere in our glen. We will seek them out and destroy them. . . . But first . . . you! You have given our Lord Mefistofelees much trouble. For that you will now perish. . . .'

Stepping closer to Badger, she raised her hands to her grinning toothless mouth.

'Sisters!' she screamed loudly. 'The wail of death. . . . Let him hear it.'

At once all the banshees began to wail. It was an eerie sight in the dull light. Their white toothless heads all drawn back as they wailed louder and louder.

'Now Beano!' thought Badger, and smiled as he saw Beano in the guise of the golden rabbit, stand up.

'Stop! Stop this at once! Don't destroy this Grey One. Stop!'

Astonished, the banshees ceased wailing and turned to gape at their golden rabbit standing on its hind legs shouting at them.

'How am I doing, master?' Beano thought.

'Pretty good, Beano,' Badger thought back, unable to keep from smiling.

'You have made me angry!' roared Beano. 'See . . .' Pointing a paw at the bottom of a clump of trees near Celan and Macgilly-cuddy, he caused them to explode. As if a bolt of lightning had hit them they crashed to the ground.

'Don't overdo it, Beano,' Badger thought, as he saw all the banshees fall on their knees and begin a soft wailing chant. Raising their arms above their heads they bowed before Beano.

'Forgive us, oh Great One. But we are only doing what our Lord Mefistofelees would wish,' the leader of the banshees croaked.

'You have made me angry, nevertheless!' Beano shouted.

'Tell us how we can seek forgiveness, oh Great God?'

'What now, master?' Beano thought.

'Order them to let me go. And explain that you will accompany me to the edge of the glen.'

'The Grey One is to be allowed go free!' Beano shouted. 'His companions are to be unharmed. I will go with them to the edge of the glen. When they are out of my domain, I will return.'

'We will accompany you, oh Great One. . . .'

'No!' screamed Beano pointing his paw at another group of trees and causing them to explode. All the banshees cowered back. 'I will go alone! I will be safe, for no one can equal my black magic.'

The leader of the banshees looked at her sisters. They nodded, then she said, 'Very well, oh Great One. We will do as you command.'

'Now!' Beano shouted. 'On your knees before me while I descend from here!'

Bowing before him, the banshees kept their glowing heads bent as Beano floated to the ground.

'Come Grey One,' he said to Badger, 'we will find your companions and I will escort you all to the edge of the glen.'

'Fooled them, master,' Beano thought delightedly.

'Fooled them, Beano,' Badger thought back, a smile on is face.

'Come on, let's hurry before they start to wise up.'

With a deep sigh of relief Macgillycuddy saw Badger and Beano come into the trees, Beano still walking on his hind legs. Moments later, with Celan clutching the golden rabbit, Badger and Macgilly-cuddy hurried towards the edge of the glen with Beano, back to his normal shape, trotting beside them.

Meanwhile back at the clearing, three beings appeared above the banshees.

'Fools! You have let the Grey One go. Lord Mefistofelees is angry!'

'But . . . High One,' the leader of the banshees shouted, 'Our Great God rabbit told us to free him.'

'Ahhhhhhhhh. . . .' screamed one of the Druids, hitting the leader of the banshees with a beam of evil magic. With loud wails the other banshees saw her disintegrate completely.

'Now get after them!' screamed the Druid who had killed the leader. 'They are stealing your god. After them!'

With loud wails, the banshees rose into the air and shot through the trees.

Badger and the rest were almost at the edge of the glen when the banshees surrounded them.

'You thought to fool us, Grey One!' one of the banshees wailed stepping towards Badger.

'Aye!' screamed another banshee. 'Let them hear the death cry, my sisters.'

Together the banshees threw back their heads and began to wail. Louder and louder it quickly grew, until it was at such a high pitch that two owls fell dead from the trees. Then as the sound grew even louder, reaching a high magical pitch, Celan and Macgillycuddy collapsed. Still wailing, one of the banshees ran over to Celan and tore the golden rabbit from his arms.

'Master,' Beano grunted as he thought. 'I'm getting stiffer . . . . help me. . . .'

'How Beano? I can hardly . . . move . . . myself. . . .'

Louder, and even louder still, the wailing grew, until in dismay Badger saw Beano fall to the ground.

'Master . . . do something. . . . '

'Beano . . . Beano. . . . '

Then a new voice came to him. A strangely familiar voice that whispered: 'the horn, you must blow it. Blow on the horn. . . .'

'The horn?' thought Badger.

'Yes, yes . . . quickly. You must blow the horn . . ,' the voice whispered and was gone.

Almost passing out, Badger grunted as he felt for the horn which hung from his shoulder. He could just get his hand to it. But he did not have the strength to raise it to his lips.

Suddenly, a tiny spurt of magic came from the belt of the Ancients. The magic ran through him and he saw his hand raise

the horn to his face. With a superhuman effort he stretched his neck, and placed his lips just inches from the horn.

Opening their toothless jaws wider, the banshees' wailing reached another high pitch and Badger could feel himself getting sleepier.

'You must blow the horn. . . . Don't let the evil ones destroy your friends. . . . Force yourself. . . . Blow the horn. . . . Blow the horn. . . . Try. . . . Try. . . .'

With another huge effort, Badger put his lips on the horn, and blew it, almost fainting. A tiny squawking sound came from it, enough to make the banshees stop wailing.

'The horn!' one of them screamed. 'Don't let him blow the horn again. . . .'

In a mad frenzy they leaped at him, but it was too late as Badger gave the horn another blow. The sound echoed around the glen.

With terrible shrieks the banshees fell to the ground.

Then Macgillycuddy who had come round shouted, 'Blow the horn again, Grey One! Finish them! Blow it as hard as you can . . . now!'

Taking a deep breath, Badger blew once again as hard as he could. The sound seemed to tear into the banshees for one by one their cloaks fell to the ground and disintegrated to dust. A wind came from nowhere lifting the cloaks off the ground, carrying them up through the trees into the sky. Happily Badger saw that Beano and Celan were alright too.

'You did it, Grey One!' Celan shouted joyfully. 'You have rid our land of the evil banshees forever. You have given us back our golden rabbit.'

'Are you all O.K?' Badger asked, looking at Beano.

'A.1, master. A.1. The plan was a good one.'

Looking around him again, Badger saw the rays from the sun pouring through the trees, lighting up the glen. Birds that once lived there before the arrival of the banshees, returned, flying joyfully through the trees and singing loudly. Squirrels popped their heads out of their holes, and once more the glen vibrated to the happy sound of the true nature of Beyond.

Later as they walked back along the path, Badger told Macgillycuddy and the others about the voice that had told him to blow the horn.

'It was the woman! The woman who give us the strawberries! It was her voice. I'm sure of it!' Badger said.

Macgillycuddy smiled a secret smile, but he said nothing.

Later on, when they came to a junction along the path, Macgillycuddy said, 'Grey One, the next task calls for all your magic. I think you should send Celan back to his village with the rabbit. The rabbit will protect him until he gets there.'

At that, Celan shouted his objections.

'But Grey One . . . I want to go with you. I . . . I. . . .'

Putting his hand on the golden skinned Celan, Badger said softly, 'No Celan, Mac is right. I know I have to face things that will take up all my concentration. I can't be worrying about you. It would weaken me. . . . Can't you see that. . . ?'

Celan looked at him, tears in his eyes. He nodded sadly as Badger went on, 'Celan, I want to thank you for your help. Without you we wouldn't have been able to get this far. Take the golden rabbit back to your village. Tell your friends I will visit them again, when the tasks are over and I have faced Mefistofelees.'

Celan sniffed, then grabbed Badger's hand and shook it hard. Then he patted Beano on the head. With a frown at Macgillycuddy he turned and headed towards his village.

'Goodbye, Grey One!' he shouted without turning around. 'Good luck on your next task.'

He'll need it, thought Macgillycuddy as they watched Celan round the corner.

Chapter Fourteen

Wondering about the next task, Badger and Beano followed the leprechaun through winding scented paths. Badger had decided not to ask Macgillycuddy where they were heading. As he walked he thought about his father, who would surely be very worried by now.

'He'll understand, master,' Beano thought, interrupting.

'How will he, Beano? Do you think that if I told my father that you and I stepped into a giant magic mushroom, and that I was given a magic belt, he would believe me? And what about all the things that have happened to us? Do you really think he would believe me?'

Beano looked up at his master's troubled face, but said nothing. He was silent for the rest of the journey.

Meanwhile, in a hidden fissure at the bottom of a mountain three beings hovered in the damp place, discussing Badger.

'Now is the time to destroy him. These tasks are making him stronger . . . building up his magical power. We must attack him together. Our lord Mefistofelees wants the Grey One stopped.'

The Druid who had spoken watched out of the corner of his eye as a tiny red spider crawled up the damp rocky wall. Closing one eye the Druid made a thin beam of evil magic shoot from his other eye, hitting the unfortunate spider and instantly evaporating it.

One of the other Druids hovered closer to him saying in a croaking voice, 'Why not wait? The angels will finish him. Let us wait and see if he returns from the Inner World. How can he hope to defeat the angels of death?'

'No!' the first Druid screamed. 'If he does defeat the angels, he will have more power than the three of us put together. We would have no chance against him. He would seek us out and annihilate us. No! I say we take him now . . . together . . . Build up our magic and have a battle to the death with him.'

'I agree,' said the third Druid.

'We have to have one final battle with him. We can use all the Mefistoes. They are expendable. They can keep the Grey One and his Familiar busy and drain him of his magic. It will be easy to overcome him if we plan the battle well. Lord Mefistofelees will be pleased if we destroy the Grey One.'

'We would need to build up our power more than ever before,' the second Druid said quietly.

The other two looked at him, smiling through mouths that had no inside.

'You agree then?' they hissed together.

'Yes . . . I have to. If we do defeat the accursed Grey One, Lord Mefistofelees will be so pleased he will elevate us to a higher magic. We might be allowed to rule this land any way we want to.'

'Yessss,' hissed the other two.

'Join hands then,' croaked one of the Druids, 'attune our magic to its highest power ever. . . .'

Immediately, hovering in a triangle upside down, the Druids joined hands, and the damp fissure was almost at once dried out as it filled with a burning light. Whizzing around and around until they were almost invisible, the dynamo of druid magic charged them with invincible magical power. Seconds later, their whole being glowed with magic, and as one they burst through the solid rock, and soared many miles to a hill on which stood the Portal to the Inner World.

Chapter Fifteen

The Portal to Inner World stood on a flat, rocky platform on a tiny hill. The entrance was through two huge obelisks of twisted rock, twenty metres high and ten metres apart. On top of the obelisks a two hundred tonne lintel of black marble rested. The doorway into Inner World was a black swirling mist. No grass grew on the hill, and the dull brown clay throbbed with evil as Badger, Beano and Macgillycuddy rounded the corner. At once the belt of the Ancients vibrated so hard that Badger lifted off the ground.

'Master,' gasped Beano.

Then Badger and Macgillycuddy saw them too.

Standing, waiting for them at the bottom of the hill were one thousand Mefistoes, saliva dripping from their horrible mouths as they watched their quarry. All the Mefistoes were smiling: cruel, wicked smiles.

'THRALLS!' gasped Macgillycuddy, pointing to one hundred fierce two-headed creatures that were the size of lions and had two dogs' heads. Each head had one huge eye which glared angrily as they barked showing several rows of sharp yellow teeth. Five Mefistoes restrained each Thrall as they roared and slavered, trying to get free to attack Badger and his companions.

All this was enough to make Badger feel afraid, but then he saw the Druids floating in mid-air halfway up the hill.

As Macgillycuddy drew his shillelagh, his heart thumped with fear as he thought, surely we will all be destroyed. He gulped as he looked again at the Thralls.

Badger's shaky voice made him feel even more afraid as he shouted instructions to Beano.

'Beano, you stay beside me . . . Mac . . . you leave the fighting to us.'

The leprechaun stared at Badger and Beano as the glow of good magic buzzed from one to the other and back again. Then, with a loud pop, it stopped, and the glow vanished. The diamond on the belt of the Ancients now glowed black again. Macgillycuddy saw the smile on Badger's face and he felt a bit easier. Beano stood as tall as he could, his tail straight out. He was ready for the conflict ahead of him . . . and then it came.

From halfway up the hill, a voice boomed out,

'Set the Thralls on them!'

Pulling at their leashes, the Mefistoes released them and snarling terrifyingly they rushed towards the three.

'Mac, get away back!' Badger ordered.

Macgillycuddy gratefully darted behind a rock. One of the Druids smiled as he spotted him.

'We'll handle the Thralls,' screamed Badger.

'Let me do it, master,' Beano thought.

'O.K. Beano, they're all yours.'

The Thralls were almost upon them when Beano began to grow and grow. . . .

Startled, the horrible beasts skidded to a halt, their angry growling subsiding as they gaped at the terrifying animal Beano had become.

Beano had grown into a one hundred tentacled creature with three huge eyes. Each eye sat like a giant marble on a quivering mass of glob. He was thirty metres high and green all over, right to the top of his suckered tentacles, which quickly reached for the surprised Thralls. They struggled in vain as the crushing tentacles held their ferocious heads together.

Suddenly, with one loud roar Beano flung the Thralls high into the sky. Two thousand and thirteen eyes watched as they flew up and up. One thousand Mefistoes scattered as the Thralls fell to the ground killing fifty of the evil little men at once. In an instant Beano had returned to normal.

'How was that master?' he thought, barking happily.

'Pretty good, Beano. Now how about leaving the Mefistoes to me?'

'To you? But, master, there are hundreds of them.'

'Yes,' Badger thought, turning and smiling at him.

Just then the booming voice of one of the Druids shouted, 'Attack! Attack! Cut them down. . . . Destroy them. . . . Attack!'

Hiding behind the rock, Macgillycuddy shook with fear as he saw the Mefistoes advance towards Badger and Beano. In lines of a hundred, they spread out. Each hundred had different weapons, and some of them had their curved daggers. With horrible screeches they stopped twenty metres from Badger and Beano on a command from the Druids.

'Master, I can change into. . . .'

'No, Beano, let me handle them,' Badger thought, an excited look on his face. 'I'm going to enjoy this.'

Two hundred Mefistoes stepped nearer, swinging leather thongs around and around above their horned heads. In each catapult was a round spiked steel ball. Suddenly, with a single whoosh they flung the balls at Badger who had stepped in front of Beano.

For a second, he stood perfectly still, the magic still working through him. Then, two hundred beams burst from all over his body hitting the balls when they were only a metre away from him. In amazement, the Mefistoes saw their terrible missiles turn to dust and scatter in the light breeze.

Quickly, another two hundred Mefistoes pushed roughly forward and, with tiny bows drawn back, they fired. Two hundred golden arrows with barbed poisonous tips flew at Badger.

Once again, he stood perfectly still, until it seemed as if the arrows would stick into him. Then quick as a flash he snapped his fingers and pointed one forefinger at the deadly arrows. To the Mefistoes' astonishment the arrows turned from their target and shot straight up into the sky until they were out of sight. For a second, Badger pointed his forefinger at the sky, a loud whizzing was heard, as two hundred arrows came from the sky and stuck straight into the heads of the Mefistoes who had just fired them.

Then Badger smiled as another two hundred Mefistoes stepped forward.

In their mouths these Mefistoes had long tubes, containing poisoned darts. As they took a deep breath to blow their darts at Badger, he pointed a finger at them. Macgillycuddy smiled as he saw the horrified looks on two hundred Mefistoes' faces as they swallowed their darts. Dropping the blow pipes they fell to the ground, dead in seconds.

So, thought Macgillycuddy, the Grey One realises that the Mefi-stoes have to be destroyed. Now, with many of their number dead, the Mefistoes were in a panic. Turning they looked at the Druids.

'Attack them! Kill them all! Attack them now!' the voice boomed from the three Druids. 'Use your daggers, use your chains, use your spiked shillelaghs . . . use anything . . . destroy them . . . destroy them!'

Snarling, the remaining Mefistoes rushed towards Badger and Beano. The nearest one hundred died instantly as a wall of pure magic hit them.

Now Badger moved towards them using his fingers like a gun. Firing beams of magic he melted a hundred Mefistoes' daggers, then caused another hundred to stab themselves. Finally, when he was surrounded by the rest of the evil leprechauns, he pointed all his fingers and revolved on the spot. Beano woofed happily and Macgillycuddy clapped and danced excitedly as they saw the rest of the Mefistoes, with their horns melting over their faces, die screaming in agony.

For a few moments there was complete silence. Then, Badger held both his arms out over the dead Mefistoes and one by one they disappeared.

'Great . . . Oh great master. I couldn't have done better myself,' Beano thought happily. 'What a battle.'

Badger smiled as he watched Beano roll over and over on the grass. But his smile faded as he heard the voice behind him.

'Grey One. . . .'

Turning, Badger and Beano gasped as they saw the Druids floating in the air. They had Macgillycuddy. He was lying flat in mid-air with a huge, sharp bladed sword, just inches from his thin neck. Quickly Badger raised his hand, but. . . .

'If you do anything, Grey One, the accursed little man is finished. . . .'

Slowly, breathing heavily, Badger dropped his hands by his side, and the Druids relaxed. Suddenly, two quick beams burst from Badger's eyes catching the Druids off guard. One of the magic beams hit the sword, shattering it into tiny pieces. Another beam encircled Macgillycuddy and whipped him back beside Badger and Beano.

'Now Druids!' Badger screamed. 'This fight is between you and me. Your existence in this land will soon be over!'

Raw magic, evil and good, erupted from Badger and the Druids at the same time. So fierce was the barrage that Beano and Macgillycuddy ran to the rocks and stayed there. They watched as the Druids and Badger built a wall of electric magic ten metres wide and five metres high between them. On the Druids' side it was black, and on Badger's side it was a shimmering white.

First it moved towards Badger, then back towards the Druids. Back and forth, back and forth, until Beano and Macgillycuddy could see that Badger was weakening. Beads of sweat stood out on his pale face as he stood with his hands held straight out, allowing the magic to flow from him into the wall. The Druids too held their six arms out, their expressionless faces just visible under their hoods.

Suddenly the wall moved right up to Badger. He stopped it with a great effort, and it wavered about a metre in front of him. Beano tried to see his master's face.

'Master, do you want me to. . . ?'

'No! . . . Nooooo!' Badger shouted, sweat beginning to run down his face. Very afraid now, Beano saw the wall move more than a half a metre closer to his master.

When Badger thought the fight was nearly lost, he saw a thin beam of magic flow from the black diamond on the belt of the Ancients. The beam hit the wall and began to grow thicker and thicker. Now, Macgillycuddy and Beano saw the wall move quickly towards the evil Druids. In a panic they moved back, one of them dropping his arms. Then the wall surged forward, enveloping the three of them. With horrible screams of terror they were destroyed. Immediately the wall disappeared.

'Hurray . . . Hurray . . .' shouted Macgillycuddy doing a little dance of joy and clapping his hands at the same time. Beano looked at his smiling, relieved master.

'You did it, master. You did it,' he thought happily.

'Yes, Beano, I did it. I didn't think I could, but I did it.'

High above them, near the entrance to Inner World, a smiling woman with a grey streak in her hair vanished.

Chapter Sixteen

At the bottom of the hill, Badger, Beano and Macgillycuddy sat by a clear stream. Beano felt refreshed after a long cool drink of the sparkling water. He shook water droplets from his head, watching as Macgillycuddy gave Badger a drink from his leather flask. As Badger drank the strange, pleasant tasting drink, Macgillycuddy said, 'When you have rested enough, Grey One, we will climb the hill and enter through the Portal to the Inner World.'

Handing him back the flask, Badger rose to his feet saying, 'I'm rested now, Mac. Let's get on. I feel my purpose here in this land is nearly over.'

'In this land, yes, Grey One,' Macgillycuddy said quietly.

Badger looked up at the Portal on top of the hill and said, as Macgillycuddy stood up beside him, 'This Portal to the Inner World, what exactly is it?'

'It is a place where the children wait. . . .'

'Children. . . . What children? What are they waiting for?' Badger asked, looking at Beano with a frown on his face. 'What do you mean?'

'You will find out soon enough,' Macgillycuddy said mysteriously. 'Come, let us climb.'

Minutes later, the three of them stood in front of the misty entrance to the Inner World. Looking into the mist, Badger shivered with excitement.

'Well, let's go!' he shouted. 'What are we waiting for? Come on!' With that he stepped into the swirling black mist and disappeared.

Beano looked at the little leprechaun for a few seconds, then he followed his master into the mist. Macgillycuddy quickly followed Beano. Seconds later, as they came out of the mist on the other side, they saw they were standing by some palm trees. Curving away from them was a yellowy-white, flat beach. The beach was lapped by a tranquil blue-green sea. Tropical birds of every colour sang in the many palm trees that bordered the beach. Parrots, parakeets, macaws and humming birds flew from the trees out over the beach and back again. Almost out of sight in the hazy warm mist at the far end of the beach, the turrets of a dark castle could be seen. The sky was a glorious cloudless pink.

'It's just like a picture postcard,' Badger thought. 'I feel so happy.' He glanced at Beano. He too looked happy. 'I am, master,' Beano thought, his tail wagging vigorously.

Suddenly, along the beach, shapes came running out from the trees. Down to the water they ran with happy singing voices. 'Voices of . . . Children,' Macgillycuddy said smiling. 'Come, let us greet them.'

As they walked along the beach, some of the children spotted Badger and the rest and all began running towards him.

In seconds, they were surrounded by dozens of beautiful happy faced children. The joy on their faces at seeing Badger, Beano and Macgillycuddy was so great that Badger felt like crying with happiness. He could feel the goodness of the children. Then one of them spoke. 'Hallo Badger. Is this Beano?'

The boy who had spoken was almost as big as Badger. Like all the children, he wore a white kimono covering only one shoulder. On the chest of the kimono was a tiny red cross.

Beano wagged his tail, as the boy petted him on the head. He too felt the inexplicable thrill of goodness from the boy's touch.

'Beano is a lovely dog,' said the boy. 'I had a dog once.'

Badger could see the sadness in his eyes.

'What did you call him?' inquired Badger.

'Laddy. He was a big brown and white chested boxer.'

'What happened to him?' Badger asked, immediately regretting the question.

'Happened to him? Why nothing happened to him,' the boy replied, smiling again.

'Then where is he?' Badger asked looking along the beach.

'He's there, back there,' the boy said.

Badger frowned. The boy had not indicated any direction.

'Oh, in the trees, you mean?' he said pointing along the palm trees.

'No,' the boy said, looking at Badger strangely. 'There, back there. . . .'

'Where?' Badger asked, not sure what the boy meant.

'There, back there,' repeated the boy.

Then a girl with long black hair shouted excitedly, 'Let's all play in the water. Come on everyone. Come on Badger. . . .'

Beano ran about in circles barking excitedly, sand scudding up around him as the laughing children chased him.

Macgillycuddy watched it all, and as Badger was led into the water, he walked towards the palm trees again. Very soon, in the warm breeze, he fell asleep.

Badger was surprised to feel how warm the water was, and it wasn't long before he was splashing about, playing with Beano and the children. Afterwards, they played games in the sand.

Two hours later, Macgillycuddy awoke. He sat up, his beard tingling with the warning of fear.

'Grey One! . . . Grey One!' he shouted.

Badger looked up. 'Come and join us Mac,' he called happily. 'The children have some great games, I never knew they could be such fun.'

Macgillycuddy reached him in seconds, his eyes wide with fear.

'It's too late for that. Can't you feel them? . . . They're here, they're here.'

Suddenly one of the children screamed.

'Run! Run. It's them. They're back . . . run!'

Quickly all the children, their beautiful faces pale with fear, ran for the trees and were gone.

'What is it, master?' Beano asked. 'Why have the children run away?'

Badger felt the belt vibrating.

'There!' the little man shouted, pointing out to sea.

'There. . . . They come . . . Look.'

Shuddering with fear he dropped his arm and moved behind Badger.

The sky was no longer pink. It had suddenly gone grey. Far out on the horizon lightning flashed. Then they all saw them.

Flying over the stormy sea came the most evil beings Badger and the others had ever seen. He could feel more magic pumping into him, and flashing also to Beano.

With loud cries the evil creatures landed.

'The angels!' Macgillycuddy croaked, his face white with fear. He moved even closer to Badger.

There were seven men or things like men. Giants, five metres tall. Their naked bodies were covered in thick curly black hair. They all had two black horns protruding from above their foreheads. On their backs were giant bat-like wings spanning twenty metres. Their faces were horrific. Two of their black teeth stuck out, hanging over their lower lips on each side of their mouths. Their eyes had no pupils, just white eyeballs that stared ferociously under thick bushy black eyebrows. They each had three single toes curved into claws and from the fingers on their hands grew long, sharp, dirty nails.

As four of the terrible creatures stared at them, three others flew into the trees. Badger and the others heard loud crashing and then screaming.

Seconds later, the three horrible angels of death emerged. Two of them carried a girl and a boy who seemed to be dead. The third held the boy who had told Badger about his dog. He was screaming and struggling with the angel of death as they flew towards the castle.

'Save us, Badger! Save us from the angels. . . !' he called as he was carried further away.

Horrified, Badger turned to Macgillycuddy, but the little man was too terrified to speak, hypnotised with fear at the sight of the terrible monsters in front of him. Then they came nearer.

'Stay where you are!' Badger shouted, his fear vanishing.

The four angels of death stopped, smiling at each other. One of them spoke, 'So this is the Grey One. The saviour . . . Ha, ha,ha, ha . . .' The angel's horrible laughter made Beano shiver with fear. 'Well tell us, Grey One, who is going to save you?'

With a quick nod of his head a burst of evil magic shot from one of his black horns, hitting Badger and knocking him back on top of Macgillycuddy. Dazed, he watched the angels advance towards them.

'Beano!' he shouted. 'Come beside me quickly!'

In a flash Beano jumped inside the protective blue magical globe that now protected them.

'ARGGGGHHHH . . . Argggghhhhhh. . . .' In a mad fury, the angels of death tried to get at them but the power of Badger's magic was too great.

'You will never defeat my good magic!' he shouted.

Once again the angels tried in vain to break through the globe. Black magic flickered all around it as they attacked.

'Arghhhhhhhhh, it is useless,' one of the angels roared at the smiling boy and his companions.

'We will find a way to get you, Grey One. And when we do, oh when we do . . . oh, we will make you very sorry. We will bide our time, for we are very patient. Your death will be a pleasant one to watch. You will beg us to destroy you.'

Slowly, the four evil beings backed away and with loud screams they flapped their scaly wings and rose into the sky. The protective blue globe disappearing as they headed across the beach towards the castle.

Trembling slightly, Badger turned to Macgillycuddy, and shouted angrily, 'Macgillycuddy, I think it's about time you told me about that castle, and them . . . them . . . things. . . .'

Beano shivered. He had never seen his master so angry. Macgillycuddy looked away from Badger's glaring eyes.

'Calm down master,' Beano thought. 'The little man's had a terrible scare. So have I, for that matter.'

Their conversation was interrupted by the children who came running out from the trees, smiling and chattering happily as if nothing had happened. Badger looked at Beano barking happily as the children splashed him with water. 'Come on master. It's great. I've never been happier in all my life. Come on down and join us . . . wheeeeee.'

The laughter and joy from Beano's thoughts were a distraction as Badger tried to think about what had happened. Shaking his head he turned to Macgillycuddy again.

'Have those things taken the children to that castle?'

'Yes, Grey One,' Macgillycuddy whispered. 'They will be drained. . . .'

'Drained? What do you mean, drained?'

The little man did not answer. 'Look, Mac, you are trying my patience,' Badger shouted. 'Tell me what is going on? Why am I here? Tell me.'

With a heavy sigh, Macgillycuddy sat down on the fine warm sand, and Badger sat beside him.

'You see, Grey One, all the children are waiting for their parents.'

'Their parents? What do you mean? Where are they?'

'In your world.'

'In my world? Mac, I don't understand. . . .'

'The children have passed on. They are waiting for their parents to pass on too, so that they can all be together in the eternal world.'

Badger gaped at the little man as he tried to understand what he had said.

'Are you telling me that all those children are dead?'

'Not dead, Grey One. Dead is too final. No,' Macgillycuddy whispered, 'they are waiting.'

'Waiting for their mothers and fathers to die. . . .'

'Yes, if you want to put it that way.'

'But why here? Why the Inner World?'

'They were safe and happy here, until the Evil One sent the angels of death.'

Badger looked down the beach, watching as the children laughed and splashed in the water with Beano.

'It is for their very goodness that the children are condemned,' Macgillycuddy added.

'Condemned? What do you mean? . . . The angels of death,' Badger whispered, answering his own question.

'Yes. Each day at the same time they come, and carry off some children to the castle. There they drain them of their goodness. Oh they're still good, because the angels cannot take away all their goodness. So they are keeping them in the castle until the Evil One can come and destroy them.'

Badger stared at the little man for a few seconds, then looked across the beach to the castle.

'I have to go there, haven't I?' He whispered, shivering slightly.

'Yes,' Macgillycuddy answered, looking towards the castle. 'You have to go and destroy the angels of death. After that you will have to face the Evil One.'

Badger shivered once again, still looking at the dark foreboding castle.

'They'll be prepared? They'll be waiting for me?'

'Yes.'

Rising, Badger looked down the beach at the children playing.

'Grey One,' Macgillycuddy said standing up beside him. 'There is a room in the castle where the angels never enter. The crystal cross of life lies in that room. You must find it first. For without it, you will have no chance of destroying the evil one.'

'The cross of life,' Badger murmured, his thoughts going to Beano. 'We have to go, Beano.'

Sliding to a stop at the edge of the water, Beano looked up at him. 'Do we have to, master? I'm so happy, let me stay a while longer.'

'Beano, we have to go.' Badger shivered again as he added, 'to the castle.'

'The castle? Why?'

'You know why.'

'To rescue the children?'

'Amongst other things.'

'Other things?'

'Come on, I'll explain as much as Mac has told me. Let's get to the castle.'

Barking loudly Beano ran to his master, and seconds later they headed across the beach followed by the children.

Chapter Seventeen

When they were one hundred metres from the castle, the children, with pale frightened faces, ran back along the beach. Badger scanned the turrets of the castle and thought he saw the dark movement of something watching them.

Minutes later, they cautiously approached the thick trees surrounding the castle.

'Grey One,' Macgillycuddy whispered fearfully. 'If you don't mind, I will remain here and wait until you come back out.'

'Master,' Beano thought, 'the little man is scared. After all we've been through that makes me more afraid than ever.'

'Yes, Beano, I'm afraid too. Do you want to stay with Mac? You know I have to go inside.'

'I will stay with you, master. Where you go, I go too. Besides, you need me.'

'Yes,' smiled Badger. 'I do, don't I?'

With a gruff snort Beano asked:

'Well master, are we going in now?'

Turning to Macgillycuddy, Badger whispered, 'Mac, you keep watch here. Hopefully Beano and I will be out shortly.'

With a grim worried face, the leprechaun watched them slip under the overhanging branches to the front door of the castle. Thick tree roots rising from the ground almost blocked the door. It had obviously not been opened for many years.

'Master, how are we going to get inside? Maybe we should split up? You could climb onto the walls and I'll try and magic myself through the door.'

'No Beano,' Badger thought. 'No matter what happens we stay together. If we are separated we will be weakened. Can you feel the magic going into you?'

'Yes, master, more than ever before.'

Suddenly Badger smiled, an idea coming to him.

'That's it, Beano! The angels of death will be expecting us to come in over the walls. They think we won't go the obvious way, through the door. Well, we mustn't disappoint them, must we?'

'You have a plan, master?'

'Yes, and what a plan! You remember the trick we used with the banshees? Well here's what we'll do. . . .'

The angels of death were hiding below the turrets, black saliva dripping in anticipation. Badger and Beano floated up onto the path that circled the walls and led into the upper part of the castle. From both sides of the cobbled path the evil beings leapt out, tearing at the imposters in vain as a magic globe immediately covered the boy and his dog. When they stood back, burning black magic fizzled from the angels' horns and enveloped the globe. Buzzing magic flickered everywhere.

At the same time, below, the real Badger was pointing a beam of magic at the centre of the castle door and in seconds had burned through it. Then, with a quiet chuckle Badger and the real Beano, listened to the ferocious snarling of the angels fighting above them. They still had not broken through the magic globe to get at the duplicate boy and his dog.

'Come on Beano. I don't know how long the magic globe will hold.'

Quietly he stepped through the hole in the door and into the darkness, Beano following him.

The foul smell hit them at once, and almost choking they made their way through the darkness by feeling the damp walls. At the far end of the passage, they came to a door. Light shone through the cracks, and creeping towards it Badger thought, 'Easy Beano, I think I hear voices inside.'

Peering through one of the cracks Badger saw many boys and girls. They were chained to the walls all around the huge room.

Low moans were coming from the children, and their faces were deathly pale. 'There must be a hundred of them at least,' he thought.

'A hundred,' Beano thought moving to a tiny crack near the bottom of the door. 'A hundred what?'

'Children. They're chained to the walls. Can't you see them? Come on, we're going in.'

As he tried to look through the keyhole, he noticed the key was still in the lock on the other side. Putting his hand to his head he imagined the key turning. The cranking, as the key slowly turned, made the children look at the door. Moments later, Badger and Beano stepped inside. Putting his fingers to his lips, Badger told the children to be quiet. With smiles on their hopeful faces they did as they were told.

Walking to the middle of the room he snapped his fingers. Immediately tiny beams of magic hit the chains, turning them to dust. Weak, but happy, the children gathered around him.

'We have to be very quiet,' Badger whispered. 'All of you go out that door, and on down the dark hall. Outside in the trees you'll find Macgillycuddy. You are to stay with him until we come out again. Go on now, hurry . . . but don't make noise.'

As the smiling children hurried to the door, Badger stopped one of the boys.

'Have you seen any sign of a room where the cross of life could be?' he asked him.

The boy shook his head, and said, 'No, but when the angels were bringing me here they avoided a door over there.'

Turning he pointed to a door that led deeper into the castle. Then he smiled at Badger and Beano and hurried after the other children.

'Come on, Beano. Let's go and find the room.'

At the door he twisted the black handle and pushed. The door creaked open.

As they stepped out into a passageway they saw a flight of stone steps with a shimmering white door at the top.

'Look, Beano. The cross of life has to be in there. Come on.'

Just then they heard the shout from up above. 'It's a trick. It's not the Grey One. They must be already inside the castle! Down! . . . down . . . Get them!'

They heard the noise of the terrible creatures as clawed feet scraped along the stone corridors.

Seconds later, Badger and Beano were at the door. Turning the white pearl handle Badger opened it.

The singing when they entered the room was so beautiful that Badger almost fainted with happiness. Beano was so moved by it he couldn't even think. Then they saw it.

At the far end of the white-walled shining room was a glass case about ten centimetres square. Inside on a white satin cushion which was heavily decorated in a celtic design, lay the crystal cross of life, glowing with goodness. The cross was about the same size as the emblem on the children's kimonos. It glowed ruby red. Then they heard the beautiful voice. 'RICHARD, YOU ARE HERE TO TAKE CHARGE OF THE CROSS OF LIFE. IT IS YOURS FOREVER.'

'Richard? Who is this Richard, master?'

'Be quiet, Beano. Richard is my real name.'

'But I never. . . .'

Now the voice continued. It seemed to come from every corner of the white room.

'YOU WILL NEED THE CROSS OF LIFE WHEN YOU FACE THE EVIL ONE. TAKE IT AND KEEP IT AROUND YOUR NECK. THE ONLY WAY THE CROSS CAN BE TAKEN FROM YOU IS IF YOU GIVE IT WILLINGLY TO SOMEONE. ALWAYS REMEMBER THAT NO ONE CAN TAKE IT FROM YOU. DO YOU UNDERSTAND?'

'Y . . . yes,' stammered Badger coming closer to the glass case. 'At least I think I do. Thank you. . . .'

As he came up to the case, it opened, and the glowing crystal cross of life rose and floated above his head. Gently the chain looped around his neck, and the cross dropped to the centre of his chest. At once his hair stood on end, and Beano could feel the floor vibrating underneath him as the goodness flowed into his master.

'NOW GO AND PROTECT THE CHILDREN. DESTROY THE EVIL BEASTS WITHIN THESE WALLS. THEN YOU MUST DESTROY THE EVIL CASTLE ITSELF. THE INNER WORLD MUST BE AS I MADE IT, WITHOUT EVIL.'

'Yes,' Badger whispered, with tears in his eyes. Then the voice was gone and the sacred chamber became dull and grey.

Outside, the angels of death had waited, unable to enter until now. Snarling with anger they pushed their way in.

Badger watched, unafraid as they came closer. Looking down at Beano he caused a globe of blue magic to surround him, and Beano rose into the air and floated to the far corner of the room.

Opening and closing their hands, and with black saliva dripping from their chins, they got ready to tear Badger to pieces. The crystal cross of life began to glow even brighter. It was only then that the angels saw the cross. Seven pairs of terrified white eyes stared at it.

The first angel died screaming as a beam from the cross hit it right in the middle of its hairy chest. A burning cross shape singed through and it fell to the floor, slowly beginning to dissolve.

Terribly afraid now, the other angels ran for the door, four dying as they reached the threshold. Cross shapes burned through their backs as they fell dissolving to the floor. Floating over them, Badger pursued the last two angels.

At the far end of the corridor the sixth angel died screaming, its eyes burning blood red as the cross shape ripped through its skull.

'Where is the other one?' thought Badger as he quickly climbed the steps leading above. 'Be careful, master,' thought Beano.

As Badger came through the door that led to the path around the perimeter of the castle, he was immediately bombarded with evil magic. Caught unawares he froze in horror as four giant one-hundred-legged spiders crawled quickly towards him. Then, the angel of death dropped from the sky in front of him.

Badger stared, unable to move until, Wham! Wham! Wham! Wham! In quick succession the four spiders disappeared as beams from Beano's magic hit them. With a loud roar, the angel swung around to see that Beano had passed magically through the solid floors and had floated onto the roof of the castle.

'You O.K. master?' Beano thought.

'Beano,' gasped Badger. 'Thanks. I lost my concentration for a moment, leave this to me.'

'Spoilsport,' thought Beano, then watched as the angel flapped its wings, rising into the air.

'He's escaping, master.'

'Is he,' Badger thought. 'No, I don't think so.'

When the angel of death was about fifty metres away, the burning cross ripped through its wings. As it plummeted to the beach another burning cross tore through its neck, and it was already dissolving by the time it hit the sand.

'No one could defeat you now, master. Not after this,' thought Beano happily.

'Come Beano, let us destroy this evil place. The Inner World has to be cleansed of all evil.'

Below, they heard the children cheering happily as Macgillycuddy led them along the beach to the others.

'Do you want me to do it, master?'

Badger smiled at Beano, 'Yes, you do it.'

Beano stuck out his two front paws. Immediately, a magic mist flowed from them. Down, down it went covering the castle in seconds. Then with a loud bark Beano thought, 'It's done, master.' In a puff of smoke the castle vanished and a lovely singing sound rang through the trees. Once more the happiness flowed through Badger and Beano as they floated onto the beach where they joined the others.

All that evening they played with the children, lost in a dream of perfect happiness.

Later, Macgillycuddy came to them.

'We have to go, Grey One.'

'Oh no! Why can't we stay here? It's indescribable. . . .'

Macgillycuddy looked at Badger's glowing face, saying, 'You know you can't stay.'

'But why not? I could stay here and wait for my father . . . Couldn't I?'

'You know you can't. It isn't your time, Grey One. Besides, you have to face him. Have you forgotten about the Evil One?'

'No . . . I . . . Must I really go?'

'Yes, you have to. Only when you face and beat the Evil One will the land of Beyond and the Inner World be released from evil forever.'

Sighing, Badger whispered, 'Yes, I know. I know, but can't I stay for another while longer? Just a little while?'

'Perhaps a little while,' Macgillycuddy said.

As Badger ran happily back to play with the children, Macgillycuddy watched for a while and then walked towards the shade of the trees. Time passed quickly. 'Master, I don't ever want to leave here,' Beano thought sadly.

'I need you, Beano,' Badger thought quietly, understanding Beano's sadness.

'Oh but master, please. You really don't need me anymore. Your magic is more powerful now. Nothing . . . no one could defeat you. . . .'

Badger smiled sadly at him, then thought for a few seconds, 'Beano, I do need you, but if you want to stay, then you can.'

Beano happily wagged his tail and looked around at the children, eager to get back to them.

'Thank you, master. Can I go now?'

'Would you accompany us to the Portal?'

Looking again at the singing children, Beano answered, 'O.K. master.'

Barking happily he followed Badger and Macgillycuddy back into the palm trees to the Portal. As they stood in front of it. . . . 'Goodbye, Beano,' Badger said out loud, patting Beano on the head.

'Goodbye?' Macgillycuddy said, frowning. 'What's this, goodbye?'

'Beano has decided to stay. . . .'

'What! Stay!' the little man shouted tugging nervously at his beard. 'But you will need his help. The evil one will defeat you if you don't have the help of your Familiar.'

'Mac,' Badger said quietly, 'I can't force Beano to come with us. He'll be happy here. I'll just have to face Mefistofelees without him.'

Macgillycuddy frowned as he looked at Beano, then he shrugged his narrow shoulders. Badger turned to Beano.

'Goodbye again, Beano.' Reaching out he patted Beano's head, then he turned and walked into the white mist towards the land of Beyond, Macgillycuddy following him.

Beano stared at the misty way to Beyond. Then he looked back at the children playing on the beach. I would be happy here, he thought.

In the land of Beyond Macgillycuddy said, 'What are you waiting for, Grey One? We must get on.'

'Just a few seconds, Mac.' Badger answered smiling.

Master does need me, Beano thought sadly. Then, with a loud bark he leapt into the mist and came running to Badger and Macgillycuddy. With tears in his eyes Badger bent and hugged him, as Beano licked his face.

'I knew you would come, Beano. I knew you would never let me down,' he cried.

'Yes, master, you're right. I could never let you down. But it was beautiful in there, wasn't it?'

'Yes . . . but maybe we can go back there when this is all over.'

'Oh yes, master,' Beano thought happily, licking at his master's face again.

'Come, Grey One,' Macgillycuddy said loudly. 'We have to get on. We're going back to the clearing.'

Chapter Eighteen

On their way back, they all noticed the change in the land. Happiness was even more obvious. Singing birds would drop lightly on Badger's shoulder and peck him gently on the cheek. He picked up their happy thoughts. They were thanking him for saving their land.

Now, as they came near the village of the golden ones, lions, tigers, deer and other animals followed them. Cean and Celan escorted them to the village green which was packed with cheering, happy, golden children. Badger smiled as he saw the golden rabbit sitting on a gold pedestal in the middle of the green.

Jumping up onto a table, Cean addressed the villagers. 'Today we honour the saviours of our village and the land of Beyond, Grey One and Beano. Their magic has rid our land of terrible evils. Now, with the return of our golden rabbit, we are saved. Nothing can harm us, we can sleep with peace of mind. So what say you all, when I say three cheers for the Grey One and Beano? Hip, hip, HOOORAYYYYY. Hip, hip, HOORAYYYY, Hip, hip, HOORAYYYYYYY.'

As they cheered, Badger looked at Macgillycuddy who seemed to be in a trance. He appeared to be talking to someone, in a language Badger could not understand.

Suddenly, with a little nod of his head he snapped out of the trance and looked at Badger. As the loud chattering of the golden ones buzzed through the village, he said, 'We have to go, Grey One. Mefistofelees is near. You are to leave the horn with Celan. He will be its guardian. It will be of little use to you now. The cross of life and the belt of the Ancients are the only weapons you will need. Come, let us go.'

Badger stared at Macgillycuddy.

'The little man is right, master. We have to go. I am not looking forward to facing Mefistofelees, but I'll be glad when it is all over,' thought Beano.

'We'll wait a while,' Badger said quickly. 'The villagers will soon sleep with the flowers, then we'll go.'

Macgillycuddy frowned. 'We need to go now. . . .'

'We'll wait!' Badger said, glowering at him.

Later, as the villagers, began to go to sleep, Badger had time to give Celan the horn. 'Look after it,' he said, smiling as he put it around Celan's shoulder.

Celan fingered the horn and then yawned. Ten seconds later he was fast asleep with the rest of the golden ones.

As they left the village behind, Beano said, 'We'll have to visit them again, master.'

Badger said nothing for his belt was vibrating steadily as it built up his magic. Mefistofelees is near alright, he thought.

At the river's edge they stood looking across. Then one by one the mermen appeared. Leaping up beside the bank their King said, 'I presume you need a trip across to the far bank?'

Badger nodded, smiling.

'Then come, get on board.'

Already the fifty mermen had interlinked their muscular arms and with their faces down into the water they drifted towards the bank. Badger, Beano and Macgillycuddy jumped on board.

One minute later they approached the far bank where Caliopes was waiting with one hundred of his unicorn followers. 'Your battles with the evil ones have preceded you, old boy,' he shouted. 'Well done. You must have had a spiffing time.'

On the bank, Badger and Macgillycuddy waved goodbye to the mermen, then watched as they leapt high in the air and disappeared below the surface of the water.

Quickly, they mounted Caliopes, and followed by the other unicorns, they headed along the winding path of the river bank. As they bounced along quickly, Badger thought there seemed to be a great urgency in the way they were being rushed to the clearing.

Moving through the flowery fields and the swaying grass, Badger's belt vibrated. 'Mac, I can feel the belt preparing me for Mefistofelees. When will we meet him? Where will I find him?'

'He will find you, Grey One. There is no doubt about that,' the little man replied, thinking to himself, where is he? Why is the evil one waiting?

'Is Mefistofelees in there?' Badger asked, jumping off Caliopes' back and pointing towards the mist which clouded the way to the outer world.

'I don't know, Grey One, but as I told you, he will find you. You must go on as if you are leaving this land.'

'Master,' Beano thought, looking at Macgillycuddy, 'I don't think the little man is telling the truth.'

'Neither do I, Beano.' Then Badger turned to Caliopes and his followers. 'I thank you, Caliopes, for all your help. Perhaps I'll see you again some day.'

'There's no doubt about that, dear chap. No doubt at all,' the beautiful unicorn neighed. 'Well, pip pip old chap. . . .'

Smiling, Badger saw Caliopes suddenly swing around on his hind legs letting out a loud neigh followed by, 'Tally ho!' as he galloped away followed by the other unicorns. Now the three turned back to the mist. 'Is he in there?' Badger asked, trembling.

'Yes,' said Macgillycuddy.

Leading the way into the mist Badger's eyes flashed to the diamond on the belt of the Ancients which was completely black, but the cross of life around his neck was glowing a fiery red.

Badger knew they were being watched, and as they neared the clearing ahead, they all heard the first tree crash to the ground followed by many more.

'Master,' Beano panted out loud. 'He's behind us. Mefistofelees is behind us!'

'Yes, Beano,' Badger gasped. 'Hurry, we must get to the clearing. At least there, I can see what sort of a monster we are up against.'

As they ran towards it, Badger felt uneasy. The magic from the belt appeared much weaker than usual. I wonder why, he thought, as the crashing and the terrifying roars got nearer and nearer. Then they were running into the clearing and in the middle of it they saw the magic mushroom. It was glowing white.

Now there was complete silence behind them, but they knew whatever was there was watching them.

'Well now Badger,' sang the mushroom. 'So you've had a time eh? You've saved the Inner World from the evil angels. My, you have done well. Very well indeed.'

'He hasn't faced Mefistofelees yet!' Macgillycuddy snarled, looking behind him. Then he sat down on the leafy ground. Above them the birds were silent.

'No he hasn't, has he?' the mushroom said, its freckles revolving around and around. 'Ah well, maybe some other time, Badger, eh?'

Badger studied the mushroom, then said, 'Can I go home now?' breathing a sigh of relief as he thought, I won't have to face Mefistofelees after all.

'Why certainly. All you have to do is return the belt of the Ancients to Macgillycuddy's keeping again. Hold up your hands please.'

Raising his hands skywards Badger saw the belt slide up and over his head, revolve above him for a few seconds, then float to Macgillycuddy, who, still sitting on the ground, opened his bag and pushed it inside.

As he did so, there was a loud crash as several trees fell on the edge of the clearing, making them look around.

'Mefistofelees!' gasped the mushroom growing even whiter. In seconds it disappeared into the ground. Badger, Beano and Macgillycuddy stared in horror at the creature coming towards them.

Mefistofelees stood ten metres tall. He was covered in black hair from his neck to his arrow shaped tail. His feet were white and cloven like those of a giant goat. In his left hand he held a black trident with sharp arrow-shaped points. But it was his face that Badger found the most terrifying. It had the look of sheer evil in it. Mefistofelees' eyes burned a deep red. His nose was more like a pig's snout, hairs growing from around it. On his head, he had two black horns which grew thirty centimetres up through his curly black hair.

'Yessss . . . It is I, Mefistofelees. Lord of this land and every land. Lord of all he sees, and the Master of all beings.'

His voice crackled as he spoke, the sound smacking into their ears.

'So you have finally shown yourself at last, Evil One?' Macgillycuddy spluttered, feeling very afraid.

Mefistofelees glared at the little man. Suddenly a beam of evil magic shot from one of his eyes and lifted Macgillycuddy off his feet before Badger could do anything. The leprechaun was flung high into the trees. Badger and Beano gasped.

'Master,' Beano thought. He was unable to think any further, his fear was so great.

Now Mefistofelees studied Badger. He smiled, his canine teeth glistening the colour of blood. 'So you are the chosen one?' He moved closer.' You will die soon. . . . but not yet. No, not yet. I have chosen to play with you.' He glared at the cross of life around Badger's neck. 'First of all, hand me that accursed cross of life. . . .'

'No . . . no . . . I. . . . I . . .' Badger stammered, his hand going to the glowing cross. He was numb with fear.

'Give it to me,' Mefistofelees hissed, his voice causing Beano to roll on the ground and put his two front paws over his ears.

Suddenly Badger felt calm. Very calm, and unafraid as another voice came to him.

'DON'T GIVE HIM THE CROSS. IF YOU DO THIS OF YOUR OWN FREE WILL ALL WILL BE LOST. THE EVIL ONE MUST TRY TO TAKE THE CROSS FROM YOU HIM- SELF. HE CANNOT HARM YOU AS LONG AS YOU DO NOT GIVE HIM THE CROSS.'

'Give it to me,' Mefistofelees repeated, his eyes burning into Badger's.

Badger shook his head. 'No!' he shouted. 'I will never give it to you.'

Beano barked suddenly, and jumped to his feet. 'Master, I heard a voice . . . I felt. . . .'

'Yes, Beano, I know,' Badger thought, then bravely he stepped towards Mefistofelees and shouted:

'You will never get me to give it to you. It is mine. It has been trusted to me, and I will not part with it, especially to someone as evil as you are.'

'What!' Mefistofelees roared, stepping back, amazed at the angry words of the tiny boy. Like lightning he drew back his trident shouting, 'You dare speak to the Lord of all he surveys like that! Hand over the cross or I will destroy you with this.'

Badger's eyes widened as he stared at the blue lightning that flickered across the sharp points of Mefistofelees' weapon.

'I do not fear you, Evil One, for you cannot harm me as long as I wear the cross of life!' he shouted.

Behind him, the mushroom had risen a few inches above the ground to see what was happening.

Suddenly, Mefistofelees threw his trident at Badger. Instantly a bolt of lightning flew from the crystal cross and hit the trident in mid-air. It turned to dust at once, falling in front of Beano.

'Arrrrrgggghhhhhh,' Mefistofelees roared. He glared at Badger. Then slowly his face took on the craftiest of looks, and he remained looking at Badger.

A few moments later, Macgillycuddy shinned down a tree behind Mefistofelees. With a mysterious smile on his face he came darting over to Badger and Beano. 'You alright, Mac? I was worried about you,' asked Badger.

Beano sniffed at Macgillycuddy's feet. Something was wrong. The smell wasn't right. The nice smell of Macgillycuddy was gone.

'No need to worry about me, Grey One. I think now I had better take charge of the cross.'

'Why you?' Badger asked, his eyes still on Mefistofelees, who stood motionless with a sly grin on his horrible face.

'You cannot take the cross out of the land of Beyond. I will guard it until you return,' Macgillycuddy said smiling, as he held out his hand.

Behind Badger the mushroom tried to sing, but something was preventing it.

'But what about Mefistofelees?' Badger asked. 'If I take off the cross he will kill me.'

'No he won't. Not as long as I have it,' Macgillycuddy said, reaching his hand out to Badger.

'Master,' thought Beano. 'Something isn't right. The little man doesn't smell nice.'

Badger stared straight into Mefistofelees' eyes. Something was wrong. Why was he just standing there? Suddenly Badger looked up into the trees in the direction Macgillycuddy had been thrown.

'Mac, are you there?' he shouted. A moment later, the voice came back.

'I'm alright, Grey One. Watch out for the Evil One. He has great craft.'

Turning to Mefistofelees, Badger saw the look of anger flash into his evil eyes. So, this is not the real Mac, Badger thought.

But just then, before he could stop him, the imposter Macgillycuddy sprang towards Badger's neck and tore the cross away. With a quick flick of his wrist he threw it to Mefistofelees and then the duplicate Macgillycuddy vanished.

'Ahaaaaaahhhaaaa!' Mefistofelees roared triumphantly. 'The cross is mine . . . Mine . . . Now chosen one . . . I am through playing with you. It is time you were no more.'

In a flash, burning evil magic flowed from Mefistofelees' eyes, and Badger fell to the ground beside Beano. As the terrible pain went through them, he thought, 'I'm sorry Beano. . . . It looks like the end for us. . . .'

Then just as suddenly as the pain began, it stopped. Rising, Badger looked up to see what had happened.

Standing a little to the left of the clearing was a beautiful woman with a long flowing gown. Her hair was streaked with the mark of the Grey One. When she spoke, Badger recognised her voice at once. It was the woman who had given them the strawberries.

'Evil One!' the woman cried. 'You cannot claim the cross of life as yours. It was not given to you willingly. You cannot claim it.'

'You . . .' Mefistofelees snarled, hatred twisting his horrible face grotesquely. 'So you have come to protect the chosen one. . . .'

'The cross,' the woman shouted.

'No, you cannot make me hand it to you. It now belongs to me,' Mefistofelees roared.

The cross had been lifeless and black in the palm of Mefistofelees' hand and the chain had tangled through his fingers. Suddenly a flash of good magic burst from the woman's eyes and hit Mefistofelees on the hand holding the cross. Screaming in the most horrible way he saw a blue mist envelop his hand. Then glowing red, the cross floated across the clearing to Badger. The chain looped easily around his neck, and the cross fell to his chest.

Quick as a flash, and roaring with anger, Mefistofelees pointed his finger at Badger. But before the evil beam of magic could hit him, another beam of good magic surged from the woman's eyes and stopped it.

Now horrified, Badger and the rest saw the woman and Mefistofelees face each other. The clearing flashed with thousands of beams, as they tried to get through each other's guard.

This continued for a few minutes and then Mefistofelees stood with his arms straight out, his burning eyes blazing with power. The woman's calm brown eyes forced a wall of magic towards him. Back and forth, back and forth, it went.

Badger saw the woman frown, and he noticed the beams of blue magic seemed to be losing their intensity. She's growing weaker, he thought. Mefistofelees is winning.

Back, back, back, the woman was driven until with a loud gasp she fell on one knee.

'She's done for, master,' thought Beano fearfully. 'Do something.'

'What, Beano? What can I do?'

'SAY THE WORDS.' Badger frowned as the thought came to him. 'SAY THE WORDS.' It was not Beano.

'What words, master? Who is it?'

'The words, the words I read in the lair of the Gorbear.'

'SAY THEM . . . SAY THEM . . . ' the voice persisted.

'But I can't remember them,' Badger thought. 'Beano help me, help me find the words. . . .'

'But master. . . .'

Then Beano saw the cross lift off his master's chest, rise and gently touch him on the brow. A quick burst of green magic flowed into Badger's head,

'Now I remember!' Badger shouted, 'now I remember. . . .'

The woman knelt helpless before Mefistofelees. He was just about to unleash a beam of evil magic at her. Badger yelled, pointing at Mefistofelees, 'GET THEE GONE, MEFISTOFELEES! GET THEE GONE, EVIL ONE!'

'Nooooooo arghhhhhhh,' Mefistofelees roared, writhing terribly. Then he vanished, leaving only a large singe mark on the grass.

With a smile Badger walked over to the woman and held out his hand to her. Smiling at him she rose to her feet.

'You remembered the words. You've won, Richard. You have driven the Evil One away. He will not return. I thank you. I, and all the beings who live in this land of Beyond, thank you. But now I must go.'

'Wait! Wait, don't go!' Badger cried. 'Who are you? I don't even know your name. . . .'

'Yes you do, Richard. Goodbye, I will see you again someday. . . goodbye. . . .'

'Wait! Don't go . . . are you my . . . Mother . . . Mother. . . .' Badger cried. 'Come back . . . Mother. . . .' But she was gone.

The tears ran down his pale face as he whispered, 'Mother, it was you all the time. . . .' Beano looked up at his master's sad face.

'It was my mother, Beano. It was my mother all the time . . . and I never knew. . . .'

Behind him the mushroom was singing. 'You defeated the Evil One, Badger. You won. Oh well done . . . but why are you crying?'

'My mother,' Badger whispered, wiping his eyes with the back of his hand. 'That was my mother.'

'Yes,' the mushroom sang softly. 'But you know you will see her

again. That is certain. But, come now Badger, it is time to go back. The time zone is nearly expired.'

'Time zone?' Badger asked, puzzled. 'What do you mean?'

'The time zone separates this land from your land. You see you have only been gone from your world for one hour.'

'One hour!' gasped Badger, looking at Beano.

'Yes, so hurry. Ah, here's Macgillycuddy.'

'Are you really alright, Mac?' Badger asked, staring at the leprechaun.

'Pish, pshaw, it would take more than that to finish me,' the little man snapped.

Then reaching out his hand he took Badger's.

'It was an honour to have served you, Grey One,' he said, his voice trembling. 'Maybe we will meet again someday?'

Badger gulped, holding back another tear. Then he felt the hot cross on his chest. 'What about the cross of life?'

'That has been entrusted to you, Badger,' the mushroom said. 'Neither of us, or anyone for that matter, can take it from you. It will remain invisible in your world . . . which reminds me, we must go now.'

The mushroom opened its umbrella, and Badger and Beano turned to say goodbye to Macgillycuddy. 'Goodbye, Mac. I hope we meet again someday.'

'Me too, Mac,' Beano said, and barking happily he turned and ran down the steps inside the mushroom.

'Goodbye, Grey One,' Macgillycuddy whispered sadly as Badger followed Beano down the steps.

Two minutes later, they were up and out of the mushroom and back in their own world. In the clearing the mushroom sang happily, changing colour many times. Badger looked for his cross but it was invisible.

'Oh it's there alright,' the mushroom sang. 'You won't be able to feel it, but it's there. It will always be with you . . . and now I must go. Thank you again for freeing the children, and all of us from the Evil One. If you are ever needed again, you will know. You won't see me until then. There are many worlds that might need your help you know . . . . Goodbye, Badger . . . Goodbye, Beano . . . Goodbye. . . .'

Badger and Beano watched as the mushroom disappeared into the leafy ground. When it did, it was as if there had been nothing there at all.

Badger's father looked out the window. Away up on the hills in the distance he saw the figure of a boy and his dog coming down. The white of their hair told him who it was. He smiled. Sunday was his favourite day. Whistling happily, he began to set out the dinner things. Maybe Richard and his dog will go for a walk with me this afternoon, he thought.